The Year of Awakening

Chris Cheek

2FM Limited

Consultancy and Analysis
Publishing & Communication

**Rossholme, West End, Long Preston
Skipton, North Yorkshire, BD23 4QL**

Tel: 01729 840756
e-mail: admin@two-fm.co.uk

A CIP catalogue record for this book is available
from the British Library

ISBN 978-1-9996479-2-6

Dedication

For all those who suffer arrest and imprisonment
because of their sexuality

"When I saw you I fell in love,
and you smiled because you knew."

Falstaff, Guiseppi Verdi
Librettist: Arrigo Bolto.

The Year of Awakening

London and Yorkshire, England.

July 2013.

Yorkshire, Christmas 1992.

The Year of Awakening

Prologue

Steve

"So let's go through this *again*," said Andy with a sigh. "We've got three candidates and one position to offer. We've got one applicant who's way better than the others. I really don't see what the problem is." He was my business partner and was normally the most patient of guys – but even he was getting annoyed by my hesitation about this decision.

"Look," I responded, "we're a small consultancy business about to expand our workforce at significant cost. We simply cannot afford to muck this up. The other two were very impressive as well."

"I'm sorry, Steve, you're wrong on this one," came the third voice in the room. This belonged to Barbara, our office manager and company secretary. "I think we've got to offer the job to Joshua Ashcroft. We'd be mad not to. Like Andy, I really don't understand what the problem is."

I knew precisely what the problem was, and it was not the sort of thing I could or would admit to in this room.

Josh was gorgeous and had looked so adorable at the interview that I could barely concentrate on his answers to our questions.

I glanced down at my papers to remind me. He had a shock of naturally curly chestnut hair, which he wore long. His eyes were a deep-brown colour but I had noticed at the interview that there were flecks of green and gold in them, which danced and sparkled when he laughed. He also had a way of focusing on you when you were talking that was almost uncanny, eyes widened, making you feel as if you were the only person in the whole world that he wanted to be talking with. His short beard was lighter than his hair and served to highlight his classic diamond-shaped jawline. Set into the face was a very fine Roman nose, perfectly in proportion.

I did not want to recruit him, even though he was superbly qualified; he had a doctorate in our specialist area of environmental studies. No, I *definitely* did not want to recruit him, even though he was bright, cheerful and funny. He was – as he'd told us himself – out and proud. In other words, he was a totally gorgeous young gay man.

I shivered involuntarily. I was terrified of him and didn't want him anywhere near our firm. I couldn't escape my instinctive reaction; I knew it was totally irrational but this was why we'd gone round in circles over the decision for the last hour.

I'd known and loved Andy and Barbara forever, and we'd worked together at our firm since we'd founded it together five years earlier, but I simply could not explain this feeling to them in any way that made it seem rational or credible.

We needed an extra pair of hands urgently. Andy was off on holiday for two weeks, and the weekend he got back I was flying to Australia for a month-long assignment. We almost certainly would not see each other for six weeks, so the decision really did have to be made today. *Now*, in fact. I sighed; Josh was quite clearly the best candidate, and my objections were weak, irrational and unprofessional. On the other hand...

Oh, what the hell. Bite the bullet, Frazer.

"Okay," I replied, squeezing my eyes shut. "Let's go with him."

"Thank God for that," replied Andy, sweeping up his papers. "So, Barbara, you'll do the necessary paperwork for us, love?"

"Yes, I'll get the letter off this afternoon, Andy. It's all ready."

"Great – now it's time I wasn't here. I'm due to pick Linda and the kids up in ten minutes and then we're off to the airport. Have a great time in Oz, Steve – keep in touch!"

He dashed out of the room, leaving Barbara and I sitting across the table from each other. She was looking at me quizzically. "Now what was that all about, Mr Frazer?"

I was tempted to shrug it off, but Barbara knew me too well. "I don't honestly know. It all just made me nervous, I suppose. Expanding, and all."

"Not the fact that he's gay?"

"No, no! That's not the point at all. How could I, of all people, not be supportive of that?"

"Well then, the fact that's he's stunningly good looking?"

I felt myself blushing slightly. "Nonsense, girl. What

could that possibly mean to me? It would be most unprofessional. And besides, I'm almost old enough to be his father." I didn't like the way this conversation was going, so got up to leave the room. "Now I really must go and finish getting ready for my meeting tonight."

Barbara grinned. "Hmm. Well, at least I know where we stand."

I returned to my own office and started to gather together my bits and pieces for tonight's meeting, harrumphing to myself. Why should it matter to me that there was going to be a good-looking, charming gay boy around the office? I was forty-two, for God's sake, and had nothing to offer a young man like that, even if I was prepared to do anything about my sexuality. Which I was not. Because we all knew what the outcome of that would be. So there. End of subject.

I picked up my bag and prepared to leave the building. Assuming that he accepted the job, Josh would be settled in by the time I got back from Australia in six weeks' time. We'd see what the consequences would be. At least, I suspected, life would not be dull with him around.

Chapter 1

Josh

Eight weeks later...

It was the Monday morning of my seventh week with Pearson Frazer and I was pretty pleased with the way things were going. I was enjoying the work and beginning to feel more confident that I would be able to hack it. That was exciting because it would mean that I could contribute to what the firm was trying to achieve.

All my colleagues had been friendly and welcoming. They seemed to like me and even laughed at some of my jokes. After two years stuck in a fairly solemn academic environment, the fact that people could laugh and have fun at work was an alien concept, but it was hugely enjoyable and had boosted my morale no end.

The only cloud on the horizon so far was the boss, Steve Frazer. He was still very much an unknown quantity. At my original interview, I'd felt that he didn't like me much; indeed, he had seemed quite hostile. He'd only been around the office for my first week before he flew off to Australia for a month. He had been pretty much invisible during that week, preparing for his trip, so I hadn't yet had much to do with him professionally.

During our few interactions, he'd been polite but distant, and I was still a bit nervous of him. Apart from anything else, he was physically much bigger than me – around six-two against my five-eight, and well-built without being too muscular. He clearly looked after himself and was in pretty good shape for a guy over forty. He had longish blond hair, bleached by the sun, which had brown streaks in it where darker locks showed through. Much of the time, his hair was tied back in a ponytail that gave him a vaguely piratical look.

Despite his powerful physique, he had the gentlest face, fine-boned and covered with delicately wrought skin, and the most adorable growth of beard when he forgot to shave. He had very expressive steel-blue eyes that he opened wide to make a point but then narrowed to listen to your response. A straight nose and a rounded jawline completed the picture. On the rare occasions when he smiled, his eyes sparkled and his face was transformed as two large dimples formed either side of his mouth, joining the one permanently in place on his chin. For much of the time, though, his manner was distant, and his eyes seemed dull and far away. It was as if he were looking past you and toward a far-off memory.

It all added up to a package that I found very attractive. Since my break-up with Greg four years earlier, I had increasingly been drawn to older men. At the same time, it was scary. I had already discovered from colleagues that

Steve was feared rather than liked in the office since he was prone to losing his temper and giving a severe tongue-lashing to anybody who was in range at the time. And surely he was straight – he had to be, didn't he?

This week would see his return from the other side of the world and he was walking straight into an enormous challenge for the firm. A government agency, a leading academic institution and a private-sector consortium were working together on the process of introducing a new system of environmental grants. They wanted to commission a consultancy to devise, and then implement, a grant-appraisal system. The decision on who got the contract would be based partly on numbers and partly on the quality of the bid. Called the Griffin House project after the office building where the partnership was based, it was a massive opportunity; there would be a pilot exercise initially and, if that worked okay, whoever won the work would run the appraisal system for the next three financial years. It was a seriously big contract which a small business like us would be extremely lucky to win.

In a staff meeting the previous week, Andy had mentioned that we were up against some significantly larger rivals, as well as a couple of the big four accountancy companies. It had been agreed that Steve would lead the writing and preparation of the bid, Andy said, and that I would be his number two. It was an exciting project to work on and would transform the business if we won the work. I was chuffed to bits.

We had all been given copies of the documents to study and they'd been e-mailed to Steve so that he could read them during his flight back. We had two working weeks to devise a methodology, cost it and write the bid.

From the moment Steve walked into the office that Monday morning, I knew we were in for trouble. His jaw was rigid, his eyes were steely and his expression was decidedly grim. The bags under his eyes spoke of extreme tiredness after a long flight. When he spoke at the weekly staff meeting, he surprised us all by his negativity.

"As Andy and Barbara know, I don't think we stand a cat in hell's chance of winning this contract – it almost certainly has the name of one of the big four on it. However, I have to agree that we can't afford *not* to bid, because even if we don't win we might get some sub-contract work out of it. But if we're going to succeed with that, it will depend on whether our initial bid is good enough.

"So, the object of the exercise is to make the best bid we can whilst taking as little time as possible to write it. In other words, maintain our credibility without the process pushing us into bankruptcy."

We all laughed at this though we knew what he meant; consultancies simply could not afford to spend all their time bidding for work and not winning. If they did, they would not last long in business.

Steve resumed. "So, our friend *Doctor* Josh Ashcroft and I will be working on the bid. We may need to call on others for help during the week, but we'll try to not to distract you too much from fee-earning work, eh, Josh?"

I smiled weakly and nodded, still trying to process the fact that he'd used my formal title. Was he being sarcastic? Ironic? Or just reminding people that I had a doctorate? I didn't really know but it made me uneasy.

After the meeting, he summoned me into his office for a

'brainstorming session' as he called it.

"The biggest issue we've got to solve is the methodology in the assessment," he said when we got going.

"You mean how to mix quantitative and qualitative assessments?" I asked.

"Well, yes," he replied in a sort of 'don't be so fucking obvious' tone. "We need to be able to mark their written submissions – that's often the most difficult bit."

"Why?"

"Because we ask each applicant to write 2,000 words in support of their project on the form and we never quite know what we're going to get. They can be difficult to compare."

"Well don't then," I responded.

He frowned. "What do you mean?"

"Don't give them an open invitation. Tell them to answer certain key questions and mark their answers. Then you can compare one answer with another."

Steve frowned. "But this is a grant application, not an exam."

I shrugged. "Doesn't really matter, does it? In order to compare one application with another, there's certain key information that you're going to want and you need to be able to compare answers between the applicants. If you want specific information, then ask for it. Don't mark people down for not giving you things you didn't ask for."

"But you won't get creative thinking if you put everybody in a straightjacket, *Doctor*," he responded.

Now I was sure that his use of my honorific was sarcastic. "So give them a space to be creative," I replied. "But get the information you need first." I tried to keep my tone even but it was difficult keep the irritation out of my voice.

He nodded, acknowledging the point. "So what sort of questions would you ask?"

"It depends on the information you want—'

"Well, duh...'

"If you'd let me finish—'

"Oh, pardon me, Doctor."

I rolled my eyes and gritted my teeth. I'd be damned if I was going to let him provoke me. "I was about to say that presumably we know, or will work out, what the ideal grant application should look like. Working that out will tell us what information we needed and therefore what questions to ask."

"But how do we know what our ideal is until we see it?"

"By examining the policy objectives in the grant scheme, I would have thought," I responded. "I assume there are some? Or is the whole thing just an excuse to give some taxpayers' money to green campaigners?"

Steve's eyes narrowed. I seemed to have crossed a line. Then he nodded. "Right," he said. "I'm done for the time being. I suggest you go and research the objectives and see if you can turn them into a series of questions." He glanced up. "Thanks. Good session."

I left his office feeling deflated and rather cross: deflated because of the abrupt end to the meeting, with the vague feeling that my visible irritation had been the cause, but irritated by his sarcastic and provocative tone. Surely we weren't going to work like this all the time? Wasn't rational co-operation better than spending meetings striking sparks off each other? Clearly, Steve didn't think so. I wasn't so sure.

We met again the next morning. I had gone through the policy objectives of the grant scheme and tried to see how we could convert those into criteria we could mark and therefore draft the questions that we needed to ask on the application form.

It had been a bit of a challenge, especially for somebody like me who was primarily an environmental scientist rather than a market-research specialist. Nevertheless, I was pleased with the work I had done.

Steve wasn't, though. Not to put too fine a point on it, he tore my draft to shreds. There were too many questions, he said, and they were badly phrased. We couldn't expect people to answer more than five questions. I argued. This was public money; if people wanted a slice, they'd answer as many questions as we wanted to ask them.

He shook his head. "Might have worked in the seventies, Doctor," he told me. "But not now. You'll have the regulatory impact people all over this, and they'd never have it. Go away and do it again. Remember, five questions and no more than twenty words in each."

I went away and sweated blood over the draft. I got into work the next morning absolutely exhausted. It had taken me until one in the morning to come up with a something that met his specification.

At our meeting, he looked at it, nodded, and put it on one side. "That'll do," he said. "Now, what about the assessment model?"

Despite having worked until one in the morning, there was not a single word of thanks, much less praise. I just about managed to swallow my anger.

This pattern continued for the next few days as we worked out our approach to the tasks we faced. The routine of statement and challenge got results but I found it draining. By the end of the week I was exhausted, worn down by Steve's sarcasm and his withering criticism of my initial – and sometimes subsequent – drafts. Then there was the pressure I felt to succeed. I missed the reassurance that a word of praise or thanks would have given me. So far, the only indication that my work was either acceptable or satisfactory was the fact that he hadn't made me do it again.

I told myself that it would all be worthwhile; we would come up with a contract-winning proposal at the end of this period of agony. But I was getting tired and I felt that I was not doing very well, which made me nervous as hell.

Friday came and Steve gave me two more demanding tasks to complete over the weekend, dashing any hopes I had of getting some rest and relaxation. I managed to finish both and e-mailed them on Sunday night, so that Steve could review them before our meeting in the morning.

Monday morning came. I dragged myself into the office and sat down in front of him. He was still reading my drafts and did not acknowledge my presence for a few minutes.

Eventually, he spoke. "Well, the draft of the financial section will do – though it's a bit uninspired. But the emissions stuff is no good at all."

I glared at him. "What? But that's my field! I know the content is right."

"Oh, I know it's factually correct. I can see that straight away. No more than I'd expect from you, *Doctor*."

"So what's the problem?"

"Too much information," Steve responded. "In case you've forgotten, this is a bid, not an article in an academic journal. Ninety-five per cent of what you've written there..." he gestured at my draft "...will go straight over the heads of the procurement guys who'll be assessing what we send in. There's too much detail and too many hostages to fortune. Go away and do it again – we need to look confident and knowledgeable without having our heads up our own arses."

I sighed and rubbed my hands over my face. The way I felt just then I could have cried, but I was damned if I was going to show any weakness in front of him. In that moment, though, something shifted within me. I knew that if matters did not improve, I would not be staying with Pearson Frazer. I couldn't work like this. I'd see the proposal through and then hand in my resignation.

I picked up the papers and left his office.

The Year of Awakening

Chapter 2

Steve

I didn't know what was driving me to give Josh such a hard time. I knew I was being unfair, pushing him so hard and being so sarcastic. But every time he sat opposite me in my office, something about him riled me and the sarcasm just came out of my mouth.

As he left my office that Monday morning, I wondered whether I had pushed him too far. He looked tired after working all weekend and then I added to his woes by tearing him off a strip for putting in too much detail in one key section of the draft bid. I knew I was right but a little voice inside me told me that I could have put it more kindly, been more encouraging.

Which was all very well, another voice told me, but consultancy is a tough business and the sooner he learned that, the better. He was twenty-eight, after all, a responsible adult and an expert in his field. He had to learn about being challenged and how to stand up to hostile criticism.

In truth, I realised that I also envied him his doctorate.

I'd had the opportunity to study for mine a few years ago but could spare neither the time nor the cash to do it. I resented his qualification. Yes, I knew it was unfair to him, but I couldn't really help it.

To his eternal credit, Josh had coped so far, and my approach was certainly delivering results: his work was excellent. Each time I made him redo something, he rose to the challenge. Maybe he grumbled a bit, but he went away and did exactly what I asked. So driving him hard was definitely improving the quality of the bid that was emerging.

It was easy for me to think that in the privacy of my own office; the problem was that I couldn't bring myself to say it. For some reason, every time the words 'well done' or 'thanks' sprang to my mind, they turned to ashes on my tongue and I was unable to utter them. Quite why, I didn't know – though I had to acknowledge that it was my problem, not his. It was hardly fair to him, but there it was.

My phone rang at that point and my mind immediately turned to other things.

Josh e-mailed me his revised bid text later that afternoon and I was able to give it the okay. In doing so, I managed to bring myself to add 'thanks for all the hard work' to the message. At least I could type the words even if I couldn't bring myself to say them to his face.

The redrafted text was the final piece in the jigsaw; we now had a draft document that could go for peer review to

Andy and one of our senior consultants, Luke.

Their verdict came on the Wednesday afternoon and was overwhelmingly positive, aside from highlighting the odd typo.

"It's a seriously good proposal," Andy told me. "Griffin House will be mad if they don't accept this. Well done!"

I shook my head. "Not really me," I told him. "Josh did ninety per cent of the work – I just acted as mentor and nagger-in-chief."

"Well, whatever," Andy replied. "If there's any justice in the world, we should clean up with this. If Josh did do all this, then our instincts about giving him the job were definitely right."

"Yours and Barbara's were, at any rate. I was less keen, if you remember."

"Yeah, but that was for different reasons, wasn't it?" He fixed me with a stare, defying me to deny it.

"Possibly," I grumbled.

He laughed. "Look. We both know that you think Josh is drop-dead gorgeous and that's what makes you uncomfortable. Right?"

I nodded sheepishly. I felt my cheeks redden slightly.

"Then I suggest you work out a way of getting comfortable with his presence, because his performance so far has exceeded all our expectations. He is a major asset, Steve, and we don't want to lose him."

The Year of Awakening

Chapter 3

Josh

The bid duly went in on the Friday. Apart from a pat on the shoulder from Andy and one brief 'thank you' in an e-mail from Steve, nobody said anything about it to me. I didn't know whether the bid was any good – as Steve had said on the first Monday, we had no expectation of winning and were really only submitting a proposal because Andy and he thought we ought to.

So were we just going through the motions, or what? I had no real way of telling. I thought the bid we had submitted was a strong one, competitively priced. But then again, I had only been a consultant for a few weeks, so what did I know?

All this uncertainty did little to improve my mood over the weekend, though I certainly enjoyed the rest and it did me good. I slept late on both days and spent most of Sunday hanging out with my housemates, Robbie and Malcolm. They were both on the stage and currently working, so I spent Saturday night alone. The house was peaceful and quiet – and it was bliss.

I streamed a movie on my laptop but dozed more than watched. Finally, I forced myself to sit upright and to face the decision I needed to make about my future. Was I really going to quit Pearson Frazer? I'd only been working there for a few weeks so, if I did leave, my chances of being taken on elsewhere would be pretty thin. My career as a consultant would be over virtually before it had begun.

I asked myself whether I really cared and found that the answer was a resounding yes. I liked the job, dammit, and got on really well with everybody except Steve bloody Frazer. He was a total pain in the neck – moody, introspective, sarcastic and downright stroppy. But he was also fiendishly clever and highly committed to the business and its mission.

His behaviour during the last couple of weeks had pissed me off, but I had to acknowledge that he'd been right about my work in virtually every case. What emerged from our arguments and disagreements was undoubtedly much stronger. If that was the case, surely Steve was worth putting up with? I could learn from him, enjoy looking at him, continue earning a good salary and revel in my dislike of him as a person. What was not to like about a situation like that? Well, the stress of such a demanding boss, for a start, and the damage it was doing to my self-confidence.

Meanwhile, maybe I could have a word with Barbara and ask her advice about how best to work with Steve. She'd been with the firm from day one, and worked with him for several years before that, so if anybody knew what made him tick, it was her.

I felt calmer after thinking through my dilemma and welcomed Robbie and Malcolm home from their work in a much better frame of mind. We sat drinking and joking around for an hour or so and then called it a night.

I went to sleep feeling more relaxed than I'd done for several weeks. I had a plan and I was going to stick around.

Something told me it might be a bumpy ride.

I implemented the first part of my plan just after lunch on the Monday. I stuck my head round Barbara's door. "Can you spare a minute?"

She nodded and smiled. "Come in and take a pew. What can I do for you?"

"It's a bit difficult really," I said. "But I suppose I can sum it up in one question – how am I doing?"

Barbara's face registered concern. "Well. In fact, you're doing very well. I know everybody is pleased with your work on the Griffin House bid. Why do you ask, Josh?"

"The trouble is that nobody ever says anything." I paused as she frowned. "Oh, don't get me wrong – I certainly hear about things I get wrong. But if the work I submit is accepted, then that's it. Nothing more is said. I'm afraid I find that a bit difficult – it doesn't do much for my morale, if you know what I mean."

"Do you mean to tell me that Steve has not thanked you for your efforts in the last two weeks?"

"No – at least not in person. He mentioned it in an e-mail, but only in passing."

She pressed her lips together in irritation then turned her head away, muttering 'silly bugger' quietly to herself. When she looked back at me, she said, "Josh, on behalf of

Pearson Frazer, I would like to thank you formally for all your hard work on the Griffin House bid over the last two weeks. You did a great job and the partners are immensely grateful."

I smiled. "Thanks, Barbara. That means a lot. Sorry to be a bit paranoid."

"Don't be silly, Josh. I'm sorry you had to ask – that should all have come naturally."

"Yeah, well. I just get the feeling that Steve's disliked me since the day of my first interview and he'd really rather I left. I admire his work, and he's clearly got a brain the size of a planet, but I find him difficult to read. He just makes me incredibly nervous all the time."

"Oh, you're wrong there. He doesn't dislike you at all. And he certainly would not like you to leave. Just be patient. All right?"

I nodded and left, feeling a bit better.

Chapter 4

Steve

I spent the weekend recovering. What with coming back from Australia and diving straight into the Griffin House bid, as well as keeping the pot boiling on some other projects, it had been a pretty intense couple of weeks.

On Saturday I slept late and then pottered round my flat, tidying up and cleaning. I watched a couple of old films and genuinely enjoyed the solitude. Sunday morning saw me on a good long run round Crystal Palace Park, followed by lunch with neighbours downstairs, Joan and Alex. We'd known each other for more than ten years, and it was a pleasant and relaxed afternoon.

As I returned upstairs, though, my mood started to darken. The flat now seemed empty and soulless. I envied my friends their easy companionship and shared sense of humour. Easy for them, said a voice inside me, they're straight. They fitted in easily and led what seemed to be a charmed existence with few worries. But my rational side knew that this was nonsense. Being gay did not preclude having a close relationship – I, of all people, should know that from my own youth. And as for a charmed life, I knew very well that Joan and Alex were not childless by choice and that their inability to have a family was a lasting sadness for both of them.

No, my loneliness was down to me. It was partly the result of a conscious choice and partly the consequence of events now buried deep in my past. I worried sometimes that I would never be able to let myself go, to get really close to another human being again. And then I worried that if I ever did relax and seek a relationship, I would be too old for it to matter.

I compared my uptight stance to the relaxed 'out and proud' approach which Josh adopted. He seemed as comfortable in his skin as Joan and Alex were. So why did I react so badly when Josh was in the room with me? Andy's words from Friday evening popped back into my head. Was he on the right lines? Did the fact that I thought he was 'drop-dead gorgeous' make me so uncomfortable with him? And if Andy was indeed correct, how was I going to sort it out?

Because it was clear to me that I needed to do something. The current state of affairs was unfair to Josh and made me feel rotten. And if my behaviour eventually drove him to leave, it would damage the future of our business.

I needed to think the whole thing through. If Andy's theory was correct and I got nervous because I found Josh so attractive, what could I do about it? One option was to act upon the attraction. That was certainly possible, but it would be risky and wrong: risky because Josh almost certainly would not be interested, and wrong because it was grossly unprofessional to attempt to seduce one of your employees. I would therefore be doomed to disappointment – particularly since the gap between our ages was so wide.

So the only option was to stop being attracted to him. That was easier said than done. Even sitting alone in my front room, just thinking of him made me shiver with desire – his smile, his sparkly eyes, the chestnut hair, the way his body moved. All these details were incredibly vivid even though it was forty-eight hours since I'd seen him last. He had this effect on me even at a distance in time and space. Being in the same room with him was a whole other ball game – hence the quivering confusion I felt every time it happened.

Thinking about it now, though, I had to smile. It was a long time since I had been so attracted to another human being, especially one as responsive to other people as Josh.

My attempts to rationalise my feelings were clearly going nowhere, especially if my ambition was to get rid of them altogether. As Andy had said, I had to find a way of getting comfortable in Josh's presence.

Then it struck me: what I was actually doing all the time was pushing him away, setting out to make him dislike me. Maybe if I focused instead on getting him to like me, I might calm down and develop some form of normal professional relationship. It was certainly worth a try and, who knew, it might even be enjoyable.

What I didn't know, though, was how he'd react to such a change of approach. Maybe it wouldn't matter to him, especially as I'd been so unpleasant to him for the last two weeks. There was an equal chance that he would be completely indifferent to my behaviour and show that he didn't care a twopenny damn what I thought of him. It was certainly a risk, though my instincts told me that it did matter to him.

Oh, well, I'd find out during the coming week.

In the event, a problem on one of our jobs kept me busy all day on the Monday, so I didn't actually get to see Josh other than to wish him good morning first thing. I managed to resolve the issue and calm the client down, but it took me virtually all day. I was sitting back, trying to summon the energy to pack up and go home, when Barbara came in and sat down.

"A word, if I may," she asked.

"Sure. I was just about done for the day anyway," I replied with a smile. "What can I do for you?"

"Well, I had a rather confused young man in to see me this afternoon."

"Josh?"

She nodded

"Why was he confused?"

"Because of all the mixed signals he's getting from you."

I snorted. "Mixed signals? What do you mean?"

"About his work."

"But his work is absolutely fine. He did really well last week. Surely he knows that?"

Barbara shook her head. "Apparently not. He knows when he's done things wrong because you tell him and make him do them again. But he doesn't know how you feel when you accept his work. Is it because you think it's good or barely adequate? Is he just getting by or passing with flying colours? He doesn't know because you don't tell him, Steve."

"I know." I sighed. "I was thinking about it over the weekend and Andy mentioned it on Friday as well."

"What's the problem?"

"Do you want the truth?"

"I think I can guess it already, so you might as well spill the beans."

I closed my eyes and paused. Then I took a deep breath and spoke. "I think he is absolutely beautiful. I flounder every time he's in the room with me and that makes me so flustered. Something inside me wants to push him away, make him dislike me."

She gave a short laugh. "Well, you're certainly in danger of succeeding, my love. He's terrified of you and thinks you dislike him so much that you want him to leave."

"Christ, Barbara! That's not true."

She laughed again. "You and I might know that, darling, but he sure as hell doesn't. I've tried to reassure him that you – we all – value him, but in the end only you can really sort this out."

"Crikey. What should I do?"

"For a start, make sure you appreciate him. Tell him when he's done a good job as well as a bad one. And try to get to know him. Take an interest, you know?"

"Well, not really. You know that my 'interpersonal skills' have never been up to much."

"You can say that again, darling. Look, just ask him things about his work at university, what music he likes, whether he goes to the cinema and what sort of films he sees. You know the sort of thing."

"Yes, but how does that help with his confidence in his work? Because that's the real issue, isn't it?"

"That's certainly true. But if you make him feel welcome and genuinely part of the team, that will help him to feel more confident. He'll know that we've got his back. Put simply, my dear, you've got to work as hard to get him to like you as you've been doing in trying to alienate him."

She was right of course, and only echoing all the things I had thought for myself about the situation during the previous evening. But inwardly I groaned at the prospect. There was a lot going on and the prospect of another foreign trip – this time to the States – in a few weeks' time. If I did nothing about Josh before then, there was a risk that I'd get back to find that he'd resigned in my absence. This was urgent, but I was out for the next two days, so matters would have to wait until Thursday.

If I had needed an excuse to talk to Josh on Thursday, then the Griffin House people provided it. It came in the form of half a dozen questions on our bid submission. I was already in the office when Josh arrived and I called him in straight away. He looked nervous, so I tried to reassure him.

"Take a seat, Josh. I have news for you."

"On Griffin House? Already?"

"Yeah, got an e-mail this morning with some questions on our submission," I said with a smile.

"And that's a good sign, right?"

"It is indeed. And a big surprise."

"Why surprise?" he asked.

"Two reasons. Firstly, that they're sufficiently interested in our bid to actually ask for clarifications; and secondly, that they had moved so quickly. They've only had the documents for four working days. I would have thought they'd take at least another week to read everything."

"Oh, yes. I see what you mean." He grinned. "Do you think we might have cracked it then?"

"Too soon to tell, I think – but it's definitely a good sign."

"Wow. So far, so good. That's ... awesome."

I couldn't help smiling at his reaction to the news. "I'm glad you're pleased," I remarked.

"Steve, pleased doesn't even begin to describe how I feel. All that hard work, and it might actually pay off. That really has made my day," he said with a huge grin.

"Well, you can be very proud of what you achieved," I told him.

He looked at me sharply. "*We* achieved, surely, Steve," he remarked.

I shrugged. "You did all the donkey work, Josh – and the lion's share of the thinking, too. I'm not sure I told you how impressed I was."

"No, you didn't. I had begun to wonder."

I smiled at him. "So I gather. Anyway, I wanted to say it."

"Thanks. I just need to know, occasionally, you know, how things are going. Whether or not you think I'm a total idiot."

I laughed. "Never that, Josh. Never that."

There was a short pause. We exchanged glances and things felt a bit awkward for a moment. I coughed, but he spoke first.

"So what sort of things have they asked?"

I handed him a printed copy of their e-mail. "I've forwarded you the original as well."

He read through the questions quickly and looked up with a smile. "Well, no biggie here, as the Aussies say. Do you want me to draft a response?"

"That was the general idea. Is there any chance of seeing a draft before the end of today? I'd like to get back to them tomorrow, if we can. You know, show them that we're keen and on the ball."

"Shouldn't be a problem," he replied. "How about if I come in around four-thirty?"

"That's a date."

"A date?" he asked with a grin. "That *will* be fun."

Chapter 5

Josh

I must confess that being summoned into your boss's office first thing on a Thursday morning was not my idea of a great start to a day. The period of time between Steve's summons and the start of the conversation was nerve-wracking, to say the least.

However, in the end it was probably the least worrying conversation I'd ever had with him. He seemed a different man from the brooding, introspective bloke I'd worked with two weeks earlier. This man I liked. I could start to get quite keen on somebody whose eyes sparkled like that.

Then, when he told me about the news from Griffin House, I was so happy my heart nearly burst. Maybe all that hard work would give us a victory. And even if it didn't, I did now at least have confirmation that my efforts had not been unappreciated.

I almost skipped out of his office to start drafting our response to the clarification questions and I couldn't resist a flirty response to his parting comment. He was chuckling as I left the room, and that was a very welcome sound.

So he had a sense of humour as well. Now that was progress.

As I had expected, drafting the response to the client's questions was not a difficult task. Three of the six were related to the text of the bid, primarily to the methodology statement; one was a slight ambiguity on the pricing structure, and two concerned the proposed assessment model.

Consequently, when four-thirty arrived I was able to present myself at Steve's room armed with hard copies but with drafts already e-mailed to him.

He smiled when I entered. "Hi. Got your stuff – thanks. Just a couple of issues on question six...' We spent the next ten minutes on the detail of these issues and reworked my draft to incorporate his thoughts.

At one point in the discussion I ended up on his side of the desk, leaning over his shoulder to point to something on the draft. Leaning down, I felt the warmth radiating from his body and caught the smell of his shampoo, quickly followed by the sharp citrus odour of his cologne. It was a heady moment and I lost track of the conversation for a couple of seconds. I recovered, made my point and scuttled back round to my side of the desk.

Steve looked up from the paperwork and shot me a questioning look. The corners of his mouth rose slightly into what could have been the beginnings of a smile. That set my gaydar spinning a bit; maybe my assumption that he was straight needed revising a little.

"Right, then, young Josh. If you can get those changes done, we can get the response off first thing."

I rose from my seat. "Will do."

"Great. Thanks, Josh. You know, we might even win this bloody job." He gave me a big grin as I left the room.

When I got back to my desk, my head was spinning. Christ, what had happened back there? Talk about a changed man. I definitely liked the new Steve and could see myself building a much better relationship with him. I wondered what had happened to make him change so much and whether it would last. Maybe it was just that today was a good day; tomorrow might see him revert to the moodiness of the last couple of weeks.

There was little sign of any reversion over the next week or so. There wasn't a reason for us to see much of each other as we waited for the verdict on our bid since we were not working together on any other project for the moment.

Steve's trip to the USA had been confirmed; he would be away for four weeks, starting after the following weekend. He was occupied in preparing for that. I missed both the challenge of working with him and the rather flirty tone of our last two meetings.

Then, on the Thursday before he left, the news came through: Pearson Frazer had won the Griffin House contract. We would be commissioned to carry out the pilot assessment and, if that went well, we would have a nice, big, fat, juicy government contract for the next three years.

The first I knew was the sound of whooping and hollering

from Steve's office. He and Andy had been opening the post and there was the written confirmation of the contract award.

Steve came racing across the office to my desk. "We won! We won! We fucking won!" he yelled. He gathered me into the biggest hug I'd ever had and swung me round the room. "Josh, you're a bloody marvel!"

"Hear, hear," said Andy. "Well done the pair of you!"

Barbara came across to join the celebrations and gave me a warm smile. "See, I told you were doing okay."

I beamed at her and nodded. This really was an awesome moment. "It was great to be a part of it," I said. There were handshakes and hugs all round the office and everybody talked for a few minutes, trying to come to terms with our success. Then Steve, Andy and Barbara headed towards Steve's office to work out how we were going to handle things, and especially the project inception in Steve's absence.

I went back towards my desk and was about to sit down when I heard his voice. "Josh, you need to be a part of this." He grinned at me. "You helped get us into this!"

"Oh God," I said. "I can see I'm going to get blamed every time anything goes wrong on this bloody project."

Steve laughed. "Spot on, old son. Spot on. Now get in here so that we can work out precisely how we're going to work your arse off."

We duly worked everything out. Andy would attend the inception meeting in Steve's absence, meanwhile I would prepare a schedule of data requirements for him to hand over at the meeting. I'd also work up the draft questionnaire into one that we would use in doing our survey in the target area. Once that was done, I could start on the assessment model. It was going to be a busy few weeks.

At four o'clock, Barbara appeared and dragged us into the general office. Cake and champagne awaited us.

Toasting our success was a wonderful moment; I knew I would treasure it forever. I was doing a job I loved with people I liked (yes, all of them, now), and I had contributed in however small a way to a really big success for the firm. How could life get any better than this, I wondered.

And then I found out when Steve proposed the second toast to me. "Josh, your hard work and commitment helped us to win this bid, which will be a transformational moment for Pearson Frazer. Well done and thank you."

I blushed furiously and managed to stammer out my thanks. A warm glow started in the pit of my stomach then spread to the rest of me. The glow, along with a rather soppy grin, lasted for the rest of the day.

The Year of Awakening

Chapter 6

Steve

The few days between the Griffin House victory and my departure for the USA were pretty frantic, so I didn't have the opportunity, or excuse, to spend more time with Josh, though I remained constantly aware of his presence in the office.

He was glowing, bubbling over with enthusiasm, full of gentle humour and more confident than he had been at any time since he had joined us, all brought about by his work on the bid and the success we had achieved.

Mind you, I felt pretty bullish myself. This was the biggest single contract we had won since founding the firm five years earlier. If the pilot went okay, we could expect three years of substantial steady income and the prestige that went with the victory. Because the project covered England only, it also opened up the opportunity for similar work with other devolved governments in the UK as well as other developed countries. Pearson Frazer had arrived; all we had to do now was to deliver the bloody project. Which brought me back to thinking about my favourite topic of the moment: Josh.

It was clear that he was passionately committed to our success. As a result, we had got off to a flying start. Andy reported back on a very positive inception meeting with the client. He had presented them with Josh's data requirement list and a draft questionnaire, both of which had come as a welcome surprise to them. Experience had taught me over the years that a successful consultant needs to stay one step ahead if a project is to be successful. We were certainly doing so on this job, at least so far.

The next milestone was to deliver the results of the pilot project in six weeks' time, two weeks after I got back. I would be relying on Josh to keep things moving in my absence so we could draft and submit the pilot report together by the due date. It was going to be demanding, but the timescale was achievable – just.

On a personal level, I felt more positive about my life than I had done for a long time. It was odd, really, because nothing had actually changed. I still wasn't getting laid; I was still lonely; and I was still completely at sea about the idea that I could have a relationship with anybody. And yet somehow I felt differently – more positive, more in control.

Professional success helped, of course it did. But it was more than that. Maybe it was that we now had an out-and-proud young man working for us. He was not a role model as such but he did provide a positive example. And then there was the fantasy element of it. His presence in the building seemed to give me hope for the future in a way that I had not experienced for the last twenty-odd years.

So I roused myself from my desk and wished everybody

in the office goodbye. I'd see them in four weeks. I gave Josh his own special wave and left the building.

The Year of Awakening

Chapter 7

Josh

It was getting on for six o'clock on the Thursday when it happened. Steve had been gone for almost four weeks and was due back the next day. I had missed his presence but we had been pretty frantic on the pilot project for Griffin House. I was running on schedule, though, and was looking forward to going through it with the boss.

I could still hardly believe how well the last few weeks had gone and I was feeling really confident. It was a welcome and unfamiliar sensation.

The church clock over the road struck six, bringing me back to the present and reminding me that it really was time to pack up and go home. That was the point at which my desktop made an odd noise and a warning screen came up.

> *WARNING - This file is corrupt and has been infected by a virus. You are recommended to stop working on the file and delete it without saving.*

"Oh, fuck!" I said out loud, immediately regretting it and looking round to see if anybody had heard me. Because it was so late, the office was virtually empty. Only one guy, Luke, was still around.

"Hey, Josh, what's up?"

"I've just got a message to say that my file is corrupt and I should delete it without saving."

"Wow, that's awesome! Jesus! I've told the boss three times about getting this anti-virus software updated."

"But it's the main financial model for the Griffin House job! What on earth can I do – Steve will go ape!"

"Christ! Then I'm glad I'm off tomorrow!"

The last two minutes had seen me descend from the heights of happiness and confidence back to what I'd so often been over the last six years: a nervous wreck, frightened and indecisive.

"Luke, what the hell do I do? Is there any way out of this? This could cost me my job!" The note in my voice was rising as the possible consequences whizzed through my mind.

Luke shook his head. "Steve will shout and scream, I expect, but – as you've found out – his bark is usually worse than his bite. If nothing else works, Barbara can usually calm him down. It would be really good, though, if you had a solution to offer him."

"I know. She's been really nice to me."

"Yeah, heart of gold and all that. As you've seen, she can usually peel Steve off the ceiling if he blows up. Tell her what's happened and she'll help calm him down."

"Great. Thanks, Luke. So meanwhile I'd better do what the machine tells me."

"Yes, pal," he replied. "You'll have to do the deed – we can't afford for all the other files on the system to be fucked up."

I closed the file without saving it and pressed the delete key. Faced immediately with an 'are you sure?" message, I shut my eyes, swallowed hard and pressed 'Yes'. Three weeks of project work and several days of my own time were all consigned to electronic oblivion. I felt terrible. I really wanted us all to do well on this project. Had something I had done now mucked it up completely?

"And where would I find the last backup?"

Luke grimaced. "Ah, I'm afraid that's a bit hit and miss too, like the anti-virus."

I looked at him incredulously. Throughout my academic career, the vital importance of a proper, disciplined back-up system had been drummed into me. Computers were not infallible and often broke down. A lost disk and no backup was a true recipe for disaster. If there was no backup of this file, we really were up the creek without a paddle. Still, at least they would not be able to blame me for that.

"We'd better go and look," Luke said, grinning at my horrified expression.

The Year of Awakening

Chapter 8

Steve

The month in the States had been really great but very tiring, with two conferences, a whole series of meetings and the project itself. The worst thing about the whole trip had been the journey home. Take-off from Kennedy was delayed by bad weather, so that we were twelve hours late into Heathrow, where we were the last plane allowed to land before the snow shut the place for twenty-four hours. Then there was the fun of getting back home from the airport, which had taken another two and a half hours. I arrived home completely exhausted, cold and miserable.

The homecoming too had been pretty awful: a deserted flat which – however fond of it I was – had been empty for a month. Just as it had after the Australian trip, it looked dusty, uncared for and depressing. I felt as I had on that Sunday evening before my trip – very lonely. I went straight to bed, exhausted after the month away and the shitty journey home.

As a result, I overslept the next morning and still felt

completely wiped out when I eventually dragged myself out of bed. I got ready and walked round the corner to the office. Snow still lay heavily but was already starting to melt. It was misty, and water dripped from everything. The roads and pavements were turning to the usual grey-black slush. The damp and dreary atmosphere of the day added further to the darkness of my mood.

In the office, we were distinctly thin on the ground: several people, including Barbara and Andy, had rung in to say they would be late because of the weather. Luke was on leave and a couple of others were stuck somewhere in traffic.

I made myself some coffee, sat down at my desk and switched on my laptop. There was a pile of e-mails to work through, even though I'd pretty much kept up to date whilst I'd been away, so I settled down to the task. The sheer tedium of most of the messages did little to improve my mood, but I slogged away for an hour or so until I was nearing the end of the list.

One of the final messages concerned the Griffin House project; the pilot project was due for completion in a couple of weeks. Josh had been working on it during my absence and both Andy and Barbara had kept me up to date, saying that good progress was being made. As there was nobody around to ask, I decided to review the files on the server to see how things were going.

I looked quickly at the main documentation, which was coming together quite well, and then went to open the spreadsheet model. No file. I searched in adjacent directories but still couldn't find anything. What the fuck? Without the assessment model there was no project. What the hell had happened to it?

The office had filled up by now. A few minutes earlier, I'd noticed Josh arrive. Now, as I looked up, I could see Barbara taking off her coat.

I could feel my anxiety levels rising so I went to the door of my office and shouted, "Griffin House – where's the model?"

Josh came hurrying over, face flushed and looking anxious. "Didn't you get my message?" he asked. He entered my office and shut the door.

"What message?"

'I sent you an e-mail last night before I left explaining what had happened—'

"Well, tell me now. What did happen?"

"The file was corrupted and had a virus in it, so I had to delete it."

"You did *what*?"

"Er ... I deleted it."

At that point I completely lost it. The combination of tiredness, the horrible flight, the weather and now this was too much. I told Josh that he had jeopardised the whole future of the firm; one press of a key and he'd wiped out three weeks' work. What the fucking hell was I supposed to do now? The deadline was only a couple of weeks away. He constantly tried to interrupt me to make a point, but I steamrollered him with my tirade about irresponsibility, not communicating and deleting files on his own initiative.

"But Steve—' he tried again to interrupt.

"Shut the fuck up!" I yelled, launching into another rant about how hard we'd worked to win this in the teeth of competition from the big boys of the consultancy world.

"You know what a coup this was for us – is your memory that short? Now, thanks to you, we're going to completely fuck up this job and in the process throw away five years' hard work we've put into building up this company. And it'll be your fault – somebody I didn't want to recruit in the first place."

I looked up to glare at him, just in time to see him flinch from my last remark. Josh had wilted under my onslaught. He had folded himself into a chair and had adopted an almost foetal position. He had gone very pale and was looking at me from tear-filled eyes with a look of amazement on his face.

I couldn't resist one more barb. "And God save me from weepy queens."

In an instant, the colour flooded back into his face and his eyes flashed angrily. "How fucking dare you?" he yelled.

Chapter 9

Josh

"How fucking dare you?" I yelled. "How dare you use my sexuality like that? You homophobic arsehole!"

My mind was a jumble of anger and hurt. I was blind with rage at Steve's last remark, deeply upset that the working relationship we'd been developing before his trip had seemingly been forgotten. I was amazed that anybody could behave like that, and frankly, I didn't care what he thought of me now. He'd just said that he didn't want me in the business anyway, so I had nothing to lose. That was particularly wounding given how hard I'd worked on the bid and the praise lavished on me when we won.

How *could* he say all that? Well, stuff it; I wasn't going to go without telling him what I thought of him and his dumb-ass company that couldn't even organise its own anti-virus software.

So I did. Tell him, that is. At some length and in no uncertain terms. I went through the fact that I'd e-mailed him twice the previous night and he hadn't even had the courtesy to read my messages before launching his tirade this morning. I updated him on the fact that Luke and I had searched through the backups (which were in chaos, by the way, another really stupid piece of bad management) for two hours in order to find the best and most recent copy of the model. That I'd found all the notes that both he and I had made and that I was confident (as he would have found out if he'd read the second e-mail I'd sent him last night) that we could have a working version of the model to the same standard as the deleted one by midnight tonight.

I couldn't resist the opportunity to get back at him as I prepared for my big finish. "However, since you've made it clear that you find my presence in the company so fucking obnoxious, I won't be around to finish the pilot. So you might indeed end up fucking up the Griffin House project, but there's only one person in this room whose fault that'll be, and it won't be me. And frankly, my dear, I don't give a damn."

I turned on my heel for the big exit – only to walk straight into Barbara and Andy who had slipped into the room and who immediately started to applaud. I stood rooted to the spot, open mouthed.

Barbara spoke first. "Well said, Josh! Steven James Frazer, you deserved every word of that. To condemn Josh without even reading his messages is unforgivable, and you know it. And then to scream and shout at him in such a way that the whole office could hear is a disgrace. And to cap it all, you put yourself in the position where a member of your staff thinks you're homophobic! For you, of all people, it's just unbelievable. Have you completely lost your bloody marbles, darling?"

I turned to look at Steve. His colour had gone from an

enraged red to deathly pale in a few moments. The change was extraordinary, as if somebody had thrown a switch. The blazing anger I'd seen in his eyes had been replaced by a look that resembled nothing more than that of a chastened puppy.

Barbara turned to me. "Josh, I'm sorry that you had to put up with all that. Well done for standing up to this silly sod. If you give me a few minutes, I'll come and talk to you and we'll sort out where we go from here."

I left the room and headed for the toilet, trying to calm myself down and recover from the shock of what had just happened.

In fact, it was Steve who came over half an hour later and invited me back into his office. "Christ, Josh, I'm sorry. That was unforgivable. I shouldn't have lost it like that."

I had calmed down a bit but I was still shaken by the anger I'd felt, not to mention the hurt at all the things he'd said.

"Those are the truest words you've spoken all morning," I replied coldly. He flinched at that. "So how much notice are you giving me? Or do you want me to finish today?"

"Oh, God! No. Josh, I don't want to give you notice at all."

"But you made it crystal clear in this room, about an hour ago. You didn't want me here in the first place, you said."

"I know. Josh, I'm really sorry," he replied. "It was a horrible thing to say and I certainly didn't mean it. Please don't leave."

"Okay," I said tentatively. "But do I really want to work for a homophobe with a temper, who won't listen and verbally assaults his staff? Even if he does apologise ten minutes later."

Steve held his hands up in mock surrender. "What can I say? You're right, of course. If I were you, I'd probably do and say the same." He dropped his hands to grip the edge of his desk and looked at me intently. "But please believe me about one thing: whatever I said earlier had nothing to do with homophobia. How could it be? I'm gay as well, after all. To give you any other impression was worse than dishonest."

This was certainly turning into a morning of surprises. Aside from that one brief moment in his office, there had been virtually no sign at all that Steve was anything other than straight; in fact, at times his behaviour suggested that he was rather aggressively so in an unappealing, back-slapping, sporty sort of way. Now all sorts of assumptions had to be unmade and little fantasies perhaps revisited.

Before I could respond, he spoke again. "And I loved the line from *Gone with the Wind*." He grinned.

"Thank you, kind sir." I said with a smile. "Of course I'll stay. I really love it here – everybody's been so friendly and I enjoy the work a lot. Working on the Griffin House bid with you the other week was really good fun, if challenging. We just need to work on avoiding any more Scarlett O'Hara hissy fits."

Steve frowned for a moment. I held my breath, thinking that maybe I'd gone too far, but then his face cleared and he grinned. "Seems to me that there's only one fiery redhead in this room this morning, and it isn't me! What do you say, Rhett?"

"Not a redhead," I grumbled, blushing slightly. "Chestnut, I'll give you, but I'm *so* not a redhead."

Steve laughed and that really broke the tension between us. He offered me his hand and I shook it with a smile, trying not to react to the sparks set off in my brain by touching him. For pretty much the first time since we'd met, he smiled at me with his eyes as well as his lips. I felt like I was walking on air.

The trauma of the great row left me a bit groggy, though. My natural inclination was to avoid such confrontations, especially after my failed relationship with Greg.

I'd been ready to run away and hide from Steve's onslaught – until, that is, I had lost my cool over his 'weepy queens' jibe. Even though the whole argument had ended amicably, it left me trembling and nervous. I replayed bits in my head, especially some of Steve's nastier comments. Had he really not wanted me there? He'd try to withdraw the statement but what if he had really meant it? Where would that leave me? Maybe I wasn't cut out to be a consultant after all. And so on and so forth, until I gave myself a good telling off and knuckled down to the work at hand.

As a result, I wasn't on top form as I laboured to deliver my promised recreation of the model. Barbara had packed Steve off back to his flat to recuperate from his jetlag and what had really amounted to a form of panic attack. I had promised to keep him up to date by text as the day progressed. At first he responded quickly but after the first hour and a half he stopped doing so, which I took to be a sign that he was asleep.

As the afternoon faded into the evening, I started to feel better. Making good progress, I realised that I was relishing the challenge I had set myself. By nine, the new model was nearing completion. I'd worked through everything, including the tweaks I had come up with during the previous week.

I ordered in some food and had a quick break to eat it.

Although I knew that self-praise is no recommendation, the result was, I thought, rather better than the version that I had deleted the previous night. At ten, though, I realised that one aspect was not working properly and my mood worsened again. The finances just didn't feel right and quite small changes to the inputs were creating big swings in the bottom-line result that were just not credible. After another half hour, I realised that I was not going to find the problem that night. I was too tired and my mind was just not functioning.

I sent a quick text to Steve, saying that I was almost there but that there was a problem. I needed a break, I told him. I went into the office kitchen and made myself a coffee, intending to drink it to warm myself up and to have one more attempt to solve my problem. I sat down on the sofa in Steve's office for a moment, leaned backwards and fell asleep within seconds.

Chapter 10

Steve

After Barbara had packed me off back to the flat, I tidied up and unpacked. I responded to a series of texts from Josh as they came through. I felt that I owed him that, having tried so comprehensively to wreck his self-confidence earlier that day. Then I followed orders and went back to bed. Apart from anything else, my tirade had drained whatever energy I had left. I hadn't lost it like that for a couple of years and it had been a real setback.

I slept through the rest of the afternoon and into the evening, and awoke around eleven-thirty feeling much better. I looked at my phone and followed the trail of Josh's messages as he'd progressed with the model. He'd clearly hit a snag and there'd been nothing from him for over an hour. On the other hand, he hadn't signed off, so I began to wonder if he was okay.

It was only a couple of minutes to walk round there, so I grabbed my keys, slipped on my coat and went over. Sure enough, there was Josh fast asleep. He had clearly just dropped off where he sat and wasn't even lying down properly. It was cold in the building as well – the heating must have gone off hours ago.

I kept a blanket and a couple of pillows in the cupboard for the times when I crashed out like this, so I got them out. I gently moved Josh into a more comfortable position with his head on a pillow and covered him with the blanket. He muttered in his sleep but did not wake, snuggling down contentedly. I was very business-like about it. I was determined not to stop and think how utterly beautiful he looked stretched out on the sofa. But, of course, I did. Bending over him to fix the blanket, I could barely stop myself from brushing my lips against his temple.

I went downstairs to fire the heating up and settled down to audit Josh's new model, to see if a fresh pair of eyes could find the error that had been bugging him. After a couple of hours, I was happy. His work had a clarity and a logic that was truly impressive; there was no doubt in my mind that this version was far superior to the one he'd been forced to delete the previous night. Finally, at the end of the process, I found the error he'd been struggling with. Pumping my fist in celebration, I uttered a whispered 'yes.'

A voice from behind me made me jump slightly. "Hey, Steve."

I turned round and smiled at him. "Hey, yourself. Are you okay?"

He rubbed his eyes sleepily and smiled. I nearly fainted at the simple beauty of the gesture.

"I'm sorry," he said. "I fell asleep. I got stuck and couldn't find what the problem was. I suppose I must have just keeled over."

"It's no problem. I've done an audit of the whole thing

and found the bug. You were adding instead of subtracting in one cell – easily done."

He opened his eyes wide with excitement. "Hey, well done you! That's great. It's always difficult to follow somebody else's logic in spreadsheets."

"Yeah, I reckon you've done a pretty fantastic job, Rhett."

His eyes sparkled with mischief and he responded in a Deep South accent. "Why, thank you kindly, Miss Scarlet. It's mighty kind of y'all to say so. Mighty kind."

I laughed. "Now bugger off home and get some rest, young Josh. You deserve it – well done and thank you. By the way, I'd like you to come with me to the presentation next week, if you can make it. It's about time we showed you off to some clients. Is that okay?"

The Year of Awakening

Chapter 11

Josh

"Invited to do a presentation with the boss, eh? That's seriously impressive, man," said Luke the following Monday. "I've been here two years and still only done one client meeting."

That remark and the fact that Barbara's eyebrows had almost shot off her forehead suggested that Steve's invitation to the client presentation was indeed an honour.

"He likes to do them himself," Luke explained. "Other than Andy, he doesn't trust anybody else to get it right. He learned that by experience when a couple of people royally fucked up in the very early days of the firm."

"But why me?" I asked Barbara. "Surely there are better qualified people?"

"That's as may be," she responded, "though you mustn't keep putting yourself down, you know. You do have a doctorate in all this stuff and – crucially in this case – you wrote the inception report and built the model. That's vital to field any curveball questions. Anyway, the presentation is at four and is likely to last about two and a half to three hours, which makes it a bit late for you to slog all the way home. I've agreed with Steve that you both need to stay overnight in Bristol, and I've booked you in somewhere round the corner from the station at Temple Meads."

"Thanks. I'd better sort my overnight bag out, then."

The two days prior to the presentation were spent working intensively with Steve on his script and the PowerPoint slides to go with it. There was no doubt that our row during the previous week had fundamentally changed our relationship. He listened carefully to what I had to say and incorporated my ideas in a number of places. On a couple of occasions I looked up to catch him regarding me with an odd expression on his face, but he looked away quickly each time.

We worked hard during those two days but also enjoyed ourselves. We recaptured the relationship we had been developing just before he went to the States – only now we were flirting slightly and using the lines and character names from *Gone with the Wind* in private conversation. We were not physically close, though – not like the late-night encounter in the office the previous week when I could have sworn that he was going to kiss my temple. I had felt the warmth of his breath as he leaned to tuck in the blanket, but he had then pulled away quickly.

The journey to Bristol was uneventful and the presentation to the Griffin House client went really well. I was terrified going into the room, haunted by the fear of mucking things up and saying the wrong thing. I was also, truth to tell, a little uncertain about how Steve would react if he were pushed into a corner.

In the event, I could see why Pearson Frazer was making

such a name for itself. Steve was fluent, confident and charming – such a contrast with the aggressive bundle of nerves I'd seen previously. As a consequence, what started out as a formal, rather stiff presentation ended as a much more informal dialogue about the issues involved, with their guys interested and anxious to learn.

I revelled in the atmosphere, which was rather reminiscent of my academic life, and was able to make a couple of important points to reinforce what Steve was saying. We overran so it was gone seven thirty by the time we left and past eight o'clock by the time we checked into the hotel.

Steve was in an exuberant mood all the way back in the cab, revelling in the success of the meeting. "Josh, you were great! You made some really good points in there and I could tell they were seriously impressed."

"Thanks. I actually rather enjoyed it in the end, though I don't mind admitting that I was terrified when we went in."

Steve grinned. "Yeah, I could tell. You went very pale and there was a moment when I wondered if you might keel over. What was the matter?"

"Nothing really," I said quickly. "Just some old problem with stage fright cropping up again."

"Anyway, you came through, Rhett. Well done!"

We parted at the lift and went to our rooms, agreeing to meet downstairs for dinner in half an hour.

The hotel restaurant was very much of its type: adequate

without being spectacularly good or monumentally awful. The wine was good, though, and helped us to relax after what had been a stressful few days. The meal was further enlivened by our waiter, Tyrone, who was a rather fay young man from Bath. His gaydar was obviously well attuned. He flirted with me throughout the meal, even asking me at one stage what I thought my 'boyfriend' would like to drink.

"He's not my boyfriend, he's my boss, Tyrone," I told him, blushing slightly and rolling my eyes at Steve, who responded with brief look of disappointment, I thought, quickly followed by a smirk.

"Yeah, right," said Tyrone, turning to Steve. "Well if you've got any vacancies, hon, I'm available. Who wouldn't want to do anything for a hot boss like you?"

Now it was Steve's turn to blush as I laughed out loud.

"Not at the moment, thanks, but that's certainly an offer I can't turn down lightly."

Tyrone sashayed off to get our coffee, singing a song which I recognised immediately.

"What is that tune?" asked Steve. "I'm sure I know it from somewhere."

"Ah, it's 'I'll Know When My Love Comes Along,' from *Guys and Dolls.*"

"Gosh, how on earth do you know that?"

"I was in a production at school."

"So, hidden talents, eh? Is this where you get your penchant for quoting from *Gone with the Wind*?"

"Oh, absolutely," I responded. "It was my grandmother's favourite film – she used to tell me that she'd seen it seven times during the War. She was completely *gone* on Hollywood, and passed it on to my mum who was equally stage struck. Mum's still big in our local am-dram company. I didn't stand a chance."

"So what part did you play in *Guys and Dolls*?"

"Sky Masterson. You know, 'Luck Be A Lady' and all that." I grinned at him. "I really wanted to play Miss Adelaide but there was another boy whose voice was better – it hadn't broken yet."

Steve laughed, "So no chance to be a drag queen, then?"

"No – and I'm glad, looking back. Sky's clothes were way cooler and I didn't really have the legs for the two nightclub numbers."

"So do you still do anything on stage?"

I shook my head. "No – only at karaoke nights, and then only when I'm really sloshed. I went to drama school when I was eighteen, but it didn't work out. My gran died that year and I had a difficult time ... with a boyfriend, actually. To cut a long story short, I lost my confidence. Hence the stage fright thing." I shivered at the memory of that dreadful phase in my life; even after eight years, it could still make me well up.

Steve noticed my discomfort and his eyes were full of concern. He reached across and put his hand on my wrist. "You okay? Sorry."

"No problem." It was a nice moment and cheered me up immediately. "So what about you?" I asked, disappointed to see his hand move from my wrist. "How did you come to know the film?"

"Same as you in many ways. It was my aunt who was besotted with the book and the film. I read the story when I was twelve and she took me to see the film at least twice.

We lived in the Yorkshire Dales, so going to the cinema was a real treat, and I can still remember the look of admiration on her face every time Clark Gable appeared on screen." He grinned. "I know it was perverse, but I always rather preferred Leslie Howard."

I laughed. "Well, he was very good looking in a very English sort of way. A real gentleman. Mind you, I could never really work out why he chose Melanie. I always thought she was a bit soppy."

We moved from the restaurant to the bar and sat on a couple of stools. Somehow, we ended up sitting with our knees touching and I was comforted when Steve did not withdraw. I realised that we were both feeling the effects of the alcohol on top of the adrenalin shot that we'd received earlier in the day – but, on top of that, I was revelling in Steve's company.

He returned to the subject of *Gone with the Wind.* "When I was much older, I took a close friend of mine to see it and he was bowled over, especially by that amazing scene with the wounded in Atlanta and then the fire, of course."

Suddenly, his face changed as if somebody had thrown a switch in his brain: the relaxed smile changed into a look of abject panic. Tears welled up in his eyes and his breathing became laboured. He rose from his stool.

"Steve?"

"Sorry, got to go. Thanks for your company. See you in the morning." With that, he fled the room, leaving me sitting there open-mouthed.

What the hell had just happened?

Something in our conversation had clearly triggered an unwelcome memory. The friend he was with, perhaps, or that fire in Atlanta. I had no idea but I was saddened that anybody should react like that. I felt really sorry for him; at the same time, it might help to explain his reputation for having a short fuse.

Overall, I had thoroughly enjoyed the evening and revelled in Steve's company. That was progress. On the other hand, it had merely confirmed what I knew already: I really wanted to get to know my hot boss a whole lot better.

The Year of Awakening

Chapter 12

Steve

Even after all those years, the stupidest incident could set me off and induce what was effectively a panic attack. In that case, it had been the sudden memory of taking my then-boyfriend to see *Gone with the Wind*. Suddenly, from joking with Josh I was carried back twenty-five years and sitting in a cinema with *him*, holding hands in the dark and...

I just had to get away, so I headed at full speed for the main door of the hotel. It was ridiculous, I knew, but on the other hand the feelings were real. If I ignored them, I was risking a full-on panic attack.

Once outside in the street, I breathed deeply in the fresh night air and got myself back under control. It was a shame – I had been enjoying Josh's company, and the contact between us whilst sitting on the bar stools had been ... very stimulating. It wasn't just that it was arousing, though it had been; it was that it had warmed my heart in a way that I had not experienced for a very long time.

I so wanted to get to know Josh better but that was

impossible. He would not be interested in an old saddo like me. Besides, I was nearly old enough to be his... well, you know the line.

Aside from the sudden memory, which had literally taken my breath away, I had enjoyed the evening and could still recall the excitement of our successful meeting with the Griffin House people and how proud I had been of the professional way in which Josh had conducted himself.

I went back into the hotel and walked towards my room. Yeah, all in all it had been a good day and I had achieved something good. Once there, I undressed quickly and got into bed. For once in my life I fell asleep quickly and stayed that way until the alarm woke me.

Breakfast the next morning was a touch awkward. Josh seemed too embarrassed to even look at me. I had to say something and for once the truth seemed the best option.

"I'm sorry about bailing last night. It's just that the friend – the one I took to the film ... he, er ... died shortly afterwards. Mentioning that night brought it all back for a moment. It was tough, you know?"

Josh nodded. "I thought something must have triggered a bad memory. Jesus, Steve, that's awful."

"Yeah, he was only nineteen."

I felt my eyes welling up at the memories, so it was time to change the subject. "Anyway, I thought I should give you an explanation. Sorry if it spoiled your evening."

"Thanks – for the explanation, I mean. And no, it didn't spoil the evening." He looked up and sought my eyes. "I really enjoyed being with you, Steve. I hope we can do it again."

Christ! Really? Why would he want to spend time with me?

"Well, I'm sure we will," I replied, trying to keep my voice even. "Thanks. I enjoyed it too."

We finished our breakfast in companionable silence and set off back to London. It had been a good trip.

The Year of Awakening

Chapter 13

Josh

In fact, our visit was repeated relatively quickly because the client requested another presentation from us, this time to the directors rather than the project team. Steve said that wasn't unusual in big projects like this and it was a good sign – it probably meant that we were likely to get approval for the full three-year deal. In a job of this size and importance, the board would want the final say-so.

He asked me to accompany him again and so we found ourselves on the train from Paddington exactly two weeks after the first visit. Barbara had booked us into the same hotel. When she told me, I immediately recalled sitting in the bar with Steve, our knees brushing. I felt a shiver of pleasure at the thought of it happening again – though ideally without him bailing out after ten minutes.

The presentation was basically the same as before, though we'd tweaked a couple of slides that we thought hadn't worked the previous time. In this meeting, though, the atmosphere was distinctly more formal and we certainly didn't end up having such a friendly discussion.

On the other hand, the directors listened carefully to all our points and asked some very perceptive questions. Despite sitting there freaking out with my stage fright, I even managed to answer a couple of them. Steve nodded his encouragement and smiled when I finished.

When we left the room my legs were like jelly, but we'd made it through and I hadn't made a fool of myself. Oh boy, was that something!

Steve was in another great mood when we emerged from their building and returned to the hotel, smiling, talking animatedly and wide-eyed with enthusiasm. His whole demeanour spoke of *joie de vivre.* I'd not seen him like this before and it warmed my heart to see him so happy – especially as I'd also witnessed him in the darkest of places.

We enjoyed another meal in the hotel. The lovely Tyrone was our waiter once again, so we spent a happy couple of hours flirting and joking with him.

At one point, we turned to the subject of work. "I reckon we might well have nailed that job today," Steve said. "It went so much better than I expected. The questions weren't all that tough – and, by the way, you handled the two they directed at you really well."

"Why thank you kindly. That's mighty generous of you," I responded, slipping into my southern accent to cover my embarrassment, though I could not prevent a small blush suffusing my cheeks.

Steve grinned in reply. "My pleasure."

Our eyes met during this exchange but we both looked away quickly, unwilling to delve into any relationship issues.

Steve steered the conversation away from the job and we

were once more talking about favourite films and shows. As before, we sat at the bar, knees touching, hands placed on each other's thigh or forearm for emphasis. I could happily have spent much more time with him. Eventually, as the clock moved to eleven, Steve stretched and said he'd better make a move. I agreed and we headed for the lift.

The lift reached our floor. I'd noticed when we stayed before that there was a small lounge area near the lifts, including a couple of sofas and a television. A vending machine sold drinks and ice.

"Steve, can I ask for a couple of minutes of your time?" I took his hand and guided him round the corner to the sofa.

He definitely looked puzzled. I sat down next to him and pivoted my body to focus on him. I took a couple of deep breaths and spoke. "I know this is probably inappropriate and might even be better unsaid, but I decided tonight that I can't do that. Steve, I really like you and I've so enjoyed working with you on this project. So I have two requests. One is that I'd love to spend more time with you socially, outside work."

Steve's eyes opened wide and he began to smile. Encouraged, I ploughed on. "And the second thing is that I'd really like to kiss you. Now, if possible. Sometime soon if not."

Steve's smile opened out into one of the biggest and widest I'd ever seen. The look was so … so adorable that I couldn't help but lean forward and put my lips on his, very gently. It was the best way I knew to offer him my affection. It was an amazing feeling; his lips were soft and it was a long time since I'd done this. I had forgotten how wonderful it was to be so close to another human being.

Steve responded, deepening the kiss, so that somehow our tongues became involved. I tasted red wine and chocolate from his earlier dessert, and smelled his cologne. I wanted the kiss to go on forever. But suddenly it was over and Steve once more rose abruptly from his seat.

"Sorry, I can't do this, Josh. Good night." He almost fled down the corridor and I heard his room door shut behind him.

Shit. Shit. Shit. What an idiot! Pushing it too fast – didn't stick to the plan at all. What a fucking stupid thing to do. What the hell do I do now?

I retreated to my room and threw myself on the bed, fully clothed. I lay staring up at the ceiling, trying to process all that had happened.

It was clear that Steve was not exactly repelled by me, which had to be a positive. We had spent an entertaining evening, nattering about nothing in particular and joking and flirting. If it had ended there, it would have been a pleasant memory to take home and ponder on. But it hadn't ended there – and therein lay the problem. Effectively I had tried to seduce my boss and that was both stupid and unprofessional. He had done the right thing in fleeing from me, even if I suspected that it had been for a different reason.

But, but ... oh, that kiss! It had been a joyous feeling to kiss and be kissed in such a gentle, affectionate way. Sitting on that sofa, Steve had looked so vulnerable and I had so wanted to take him properly in my arms and comfort him, make him feel good about himself. That was my main motivation at that moment, though I have to confess that I also wanted him in another way altogether – in bed, naked and inside me.

I shut my eyes. There was no point in worrying now. What was done was done and we'd see what the consequences were in the morning. Meanwhile, it was time to strip off, lie back and dream of the beautiful man that I had *almost* had in my arms tonight.

The Year of Awakening

Chapter 14

Steve

Having fled down the corridor and let myself into the room, I leant against the closed door and took several deep breaths as I tried to recover my composure. I told myself that I had been right to get out of an embarrassing situation. After all, Josh was my employee; I had a duty of care and to breach that through any form of intimacy would be grossly unprofessional. In any case, it was impossible – I was almost old enough to be his father.

And yet... He was so beautiful, and not just in his looks. He was gentle, caring, funny and clever. I felt relaxed in his company in a way that I had not done since... *don't go there, Steve* ... for a very long time. There was no doubt that I was becoming exceedingly fond of him, and – judging by tonight's events – some of that fondness was reciprocated.

But I had to be very careful. In many ways, it would be easier if he resigned and left. I could surely go back to being as I was before he joined the firm. Indeed, it was precisely the fear of this sort of problem that had led me to oppose his appointment in the first place.

I moved away from the door and decided to get ready for bed. Even if I wasn't able to sleep, I could work out a plan of action. God, I was in such trouble! I had buried all this stuff for twenty years but now the lid of the box had sprung open and everything was leaking out. I doubted whether I would ever be able to get it back inside with the lid closed again. Even more disturbingly, I was not sure I wanted to.

Josh Ashcroft had turned my life upside down completely over the past few weeks, and in many ways that was a bloody nuisance. But I couldn't regret the day he had walked into my office for his interview. Bless him.

The immediate problem was to get over the inevitable embarrassment of meeting him the next morning and travelling back to the office with him. As the older and senior man, it was my responsibility to apologise and to try to set things right. Having resolved this, I calmed down sufficiently to get some sleep.

In the event, Josh confounded me, as he so often did. He found a quiet corner in the hotel in which to have breakfast and, as soon as we had made our selections and sat down, he spoke.

"Steve, I have to apologise for last night. I took things way too far and it was wrong of me. I can promise you that such a thing will never happen again. I enjoy working with you very much and I enjoy your company. I would never willingly do anything to jeopardise that."

I couldn't help but feel a slight twinge of disappointment, but he was right, of course, and he was being very gracious about the whole thing.

"Josh, that's very kind. But I wasn't exactly blameless either, you know. I feel as if you're also owed an apology."

"Accepted, Mr Frazer, sir," he said, smiling gently and looking straight into my eyes, with a touch of wistfulness. "Actually, I wondered whether it would help our 'cooling off' period if I took a few days' leave. I know I've only been working for you for five minutes, and I'm probably not entitled to any paid time off, but the Griffin House project has been fairly intense so it would be good to have a short break. You should probably do the same."

I nodded my agreement. "That's no problem. We'll sort it out with Barbara when we get back."

We both relaxed after that and travelled back to the office together without any strain or embarrassment, resuming our rather jokey relationship. It was, I felt, more than I deserved.

At the same time, I knew that things had shifted between us. I couldn't look at Josh's face without remembering how his lips had felt on mine and without wanting the same thing to happen again.

We returned to the office and sorted out his leave. As he prepared to head out again he said, "Please let me know if you hear anything from the guys at Griffin House."

"Certainly will," I promised. "And Josh? Thanks for all your hard work on the project, and for yesterday – and for last night."

He grinned. "My pleasure, Scarlett. But thank you, too."

"Whatever for?"

"Oh, I don't know. For letting me work for you. For

being on this earth. For being you. Take your pick, really."
He winked at me.

"Silly devil. Get going, and I'll see you a week on
Monday."

The week without Josh in the office proved to be long,
boring and upsetting. The worst day was the Tuesday when
our network went down suddenly and without warning. I
was in a bad mood already after a rotten night's sleep; then
a web page I had been reading for research was suddenly
replaced by an error message.

What the fuck?

I yelled for Barbara and Luke to find out what was going
on. When they confessed that they didn't know, I went
ballistic. No sooner had they calmed me down than the
revelation that our maintenance agreement had not been
renewed set me off again. It would cost a fortune as a one-
off charge to call the engineers out, but in the end I had to
agree to it.

Eventually Barbara lost patience with me and sent
Luke off to talk to the engineers whilst she stayed put in
my office. "It's your fault, you know, all this," she said
sharply.

"What? I didn't persuade the router thingy or whatever
it is to break down!"

"No, but you refused to renew the maintenance contract
last year when it fell due."

"Well, we'd paid them all that money over the years and
never called them out. And we were a bit short of cash at

the time, if you remember."

"Yes, I know," she said. "But now you've had to call them out – and look how much you'll be paying for that."

She was certainly right there: the one-off call-out fee was higher than the whole of the previous year's premium.

"Yes, I know, I'm sorry," I said.

"And whilst we're on the subject of you, what's with all these temper tantrums today? I thought we'd got over those."

"Again, I'm sorry. All right?"

"Well no, actually," she replied looking straight into my eyes with the devastating frankness that I had loved her for all these years. "Number one, I don't want to go back to the days when the whole office walked round on tiptoes in case they upset his highness. And number two, it's not good for you. You literally went purple in the face just now. I'm afraid that one of these days you'll burst a blood vessel or something."

"I do try and I have been better lately," I replied, feeling a little shamefaced. "But I had a rotten night and then this problem this morning and then...'

I tailed off, realising what I had been about to say and not wanting to admit anything. Barbara had other ideas, and finished my sentence for me. "...And Josh isn't here."

"Well yes, actually," I responded with a small smile. "It's amazing what a difference he's made to the whole atmosphere of this place. This week seems so flat without his jokes and his presence."

"I know what you mean," she replied. "It's odd really, because you could never say that he dominated a room when he was in it, like some charismatic people do. He just enriches the atmosphere. It seems almost boring without him. Anyway, just try to keep a bit calmer, Steve, all right? He'll be back on Monday."

I grinned. "Message received."

The subject of Josh came up again the next day as the three of us sat down for our weekly project-review meeting.

"Josh definitely brightens the place up," said Andy. "It's been really dull this week."

"You too?" responded Barbara, laughing.

"He's also pretty good for us," I responded. "His work on Griffin House was amazing – and he can put it across, too. He was excellent at the two presentations."

"Have we heard any more from them?"

I shook my head. 'Not so far. I'm hoping to have some reaction before the end of the week."

"Fingers crossed," said Barbara. "But I've got some bad news on the Welsh stuff. We missed out on the job and the worrying thing is that we were beaten on price."

"Shit," said Andy. "What the hell?"

Being a small firm with low overheads, we were almost always cheaper than the bigger consultancies in our field. The problem was that if they were short of work, they would slash their prices to keep jobs coming in and the cash flowing. That was what had happened here.

We kicked the problem around for a while but didn't reach any conclusions; then we turned to the question of new work prospects. There were plenty of projects to go for, though competition was fierce. Consultancy was not a business for long-term planning and building a brand was tough. Your reputation is only as good as your last job and history was littered with firms who had forgotten that mantra and eventually gone under.

Altogether, though, it was a very positive session, despite the news from Wales. When we were done, Andy went off to visit a client. Barbara didn't move, however – a sure sign that she had something else to say.

"So how are things between you and Josh?"

"Whoa!" I responded. "Where did that come from?"

She grinned. "Well, it's moderately clear that he worships the ground you walk on. And you don't seem above making sheep's eyes every now and again."

I was dumbfounded. Had we – I – been that obvious? Crikey!

"Oh, don't worry. I don't think it's obvious to anybody else," she added hurriedly. "But after knowing you for fifteen years...'

"Understood. Phew! I am very fond of Josh and we have a lot in common. But that's where it ends," I said, recovering my composure a little. "And it's got to stay like that. I'm his boss, so it would be most unprofessional. Besides which I'm—'

"Almost old enough to be his father," she interjected. "Yes, we've heard that line before."

"Well, it's true!"

"Actually, it isn't, Steve. Fourteen years is not really a generation, you know," she responded. "But the fact is that you've been on your own for so long, and I know how wretchedly unhappy you've been at times over the years. I'd hate to see you pass up the chance of happiness for the sake of some misplaced duty to this firm or your conception of professional conduct." She paused and then added, "I do worry about you, you know."

The kindness and concern in her voice were familiar but always comforting. I felt my eyes smarting a little. "I know you do, love. And don't think it isn't appreciated. But I've worked too hard and too long to jeopardise this firm's future for the sake of a fling with a boy."

"Number one, Josh is more than a boy and you know it. He's a bright, intelligent young man who knows his own mind and who clearly thinks a lot of you. And number two, I think it's a bit more serious than a 'fling.' So you're being a bit unfair on him and on yourself, don't you think? Don't push him away ... and don't you dare hurt him, or you'll have me to answer to."

I grinned. "Yes, ma'am."

The news we had been waiting for came through on the Friday. The Griffin House people had accepted our report and endorsed our proposed methodology. This meant that we had the three-year contract to implement the scheme and to do the assessment work on all the grant applications. It was a larger guaranteed income than we had ever had in our time in business and meant that Pearson Frazer was really going somewhere. Not only had we been right to expand by taking on Josh, but we'd probably need two more people as well.

I was over the moon. As soon as Barbara, Andy and I had stopped dancing round the room, I found my phone and texted Josh.

STEVE:>> Great news! All systems go on Griffin House. Thanks so much for your contribution to this fantastic result.

He texted me straight back.

JOSH:>> OMG Am so delighted. Fantastic result, Scarlett.

STEVE:>> Much booze and celebratory dinner later. You able to join us?

JOSH:>> Try and keep me away! Just tell me when and where.

I beamed at my phone. We'd won the fucking contract *and* I was going to see Josh again, four whole days before he was due back to work.

The Year of Awakening

Chapter 15

Josh

"Why is this pavement swaying?" asked Steve.

"I dunno," I replied. "You sure it's not you that's swaying? You look a bit wobbly to me. In fact, come to think of it, you look *very* wobbly ... plus the fact that there seems to be two of you."

"Do you think we might be just the tiniest bit drunk?"

"Us? Such upright and sober citizens? Certainly not!" I replied, tripping over a paving stone. "Whoops."

Steve grabbed my arm to keep my upright and I didn't want to let him go. Ever.

We were walking home after the celebratory dinner that Barbara had hurriedly organised to mark the Griffin House victory. When I'd received Steve's text earlier in the day, his invitation had stunned me. After all, I was the most junior and recently recruited member of the team and all I'd really done was update a fucking spreadsheet. Hardly rocket science. I was immensely flattered to be asked. Whatever personal chemistry there might be between Steve and me – and there was clearly a lot – was a different matter which we would have to work out. But this was *business*, which was surely separate.

However, it became increasingly clear as the evening wore on that this was not how small businesses worked – at least not this one. Andy, Barbara and Steve were very close to each other. They had a shared outlook, shared ambitions and a willingness to support each other. Time after time their conversation showed that each instinctively understood the other and knew how they thought and felt. It was a fascinating insight into really successful teamwork. I was staggered that they had included me and really puzzled as to why.

It was a wonderful evening but getting into the fresh air brought home the reality of just how much we'd had to drink. After I tripped I hung on to Steve. He was clearly happy about that and tucked my arm into his.

Things between us had shifted again. Steve sat close to me throughout dinner and we were thigh to thigh on the restaurant's banquette for long periods. Two or three times, initially under the table but later in full view, he reached for and took my hand.

Barbara watched all this and kept smiling to herself. When the time came to head for home, she more or less insisted that I should walk Steve home. She whispered in my ear, "You will look after him for me, now, won't you?"

I nodded in reply and smiled.

The restaurant where we had spent the evening was local to the office and so also close to Steve's flat. I'd been lucky enough to get a house share just around the corner with two gay friends from undergraduate days, Robbie and Malcolm. Thus, Steve and I did not have far to walk together.

As we neared his block, I started to hum a tune quietly to myself.

"I know that tune," said Steve. "The boy in the hotel sang it the other week. From *Guys and Dolls*?" He paused. "I remember! 'I'll Know When My Love Comes Along.'"

I don't know what made me say it, but I did. "But will you?"

"Will I what?"

"Know when your love comes along?"

He looked at me intently. "I think so."

Then I kissed him. Not gently, like in Bristol the previous week, but hungrily and passionately. And he responded. It was a glorious moment as our bodies moved together. It was a long time since I had been wrapped in another human body like that, and it felt so good.

When he broke the kiss, he looked at me again and breathed my name. "Josh...'

The sound of a stranger's footsteps on the pavement disrupted the moment and we started to walk again. We reached his front door and I wondered what would happen next. I held my breath.

Steve turned to face me and looked me straight in the eye. "It's late and we're very drunk. And this is too important to happen like this. Will you come round tomorrow? About four. And stay for dinner?"

"Love too," I said, trying – and failing – to hide my disappointment. I couldn't help thinking that he was pushing me away again. But it was as if he read my mind.

"Trust me, Josh. I'm not trying to push you away. It's just ... it's just that there are things I have to tell you before..."

He cupped my face with his hand and kissed my cheek. "You have to understand what you're taking on with me."

"I understand ... I think."

"You will, Rhett, you will."

"Goodnight, Scarlett. See you tomorrow."

Chapter 16

Steve

That was some evening. Lots to celebrate about the new contract but also about my feelings for Josh. Barbara's little lecture the previous Wednesday had given me real pause for thought. She was, of course, absolutely right; it was about time that I sorted myself out and *did* something. After all, Josh had made his own feelings plain on a couple of occasions and given me the opportunity to respond to him. Which I had, up to a point.

But each time I had frozen and run away. Twenty years of loneliness and regret had kicked in and my instinct told me that this was too soon and I wasn't ready for it. On the other hand, I had come to realise that my instinct was, in fact, just fear. My abstinence had to come to an end if I was not going to throw my whole life away because of what had happened to me all those years ago.

So, I had made a plan. Needless to say, it had not included getting plastered on Friday night and making out with the man on my own doorstep. But it did include sitting Josh down and telling him how I felt about him, and asking him to help me to love him in the way he deserved and I wanted to. That would require patience and forbearance on his part and he had to be given the choice as to whether he could cope with that. My gut instinct was that he would and could – otherwise I would not be planning to ask him.

Thus it was that I seemed to be pushing him away again and I saw that in his face as I said goodnight to him on my doorstep. I was too tired and too drunk to tell him the whole story tonight; I suspected that its narration would require a good deal of emotional energy on both our parts.

Trouble was, having issued the invitation, I now could not wait for four o'clock to come and for me to see him again and hold him and ... well, who knew what might happen then?

He was prompt to the second and stood there looking adorable in a crisp white tee shirt and a stunningly tight pair of jeans. He'd obviously not long showered because his chestnut curls looked slightly damp and I could smell his shampoo as I gave him a welcome kiss.

"Well hello there, Rhett! Come away in, y'all."

"Howdy, pardner," he responded with a big grin on his face.

"You look ... amazingly sexy this afternoon."

He wriggled slightly and smiled shyly. "We aim to please. Mind you, you're not looking too bad yourself."

"Come into the front. I realised earlier that you haven't been to the flat before. Would you like the 50p tour or the £1.50 one?"

"Ooh, let me see. What's the difference then?"

"On the £1.50 tour, you get to see my bedroom."

"Oh, well," he responded, laughing. "No contest

then. The £1.50 tour it is. Especially since we have some unfinished business from last night. It got postponed for some reason – something about feeling too tired and a bit tiddly, I seem to remember. I realise that we've got to be patient with you *old* men, but..."

He came close to me and reached out to cup my chin.

"Cheeky sod," I responded, ruffling his hair. "We've got a tour to do first and then I'm afraid you've got to listen to a short lecture."

He rolled his eyes at me and pretended to groan. "A lecture? On a Saturday afternoon? What about?"

"Me," I replied, fixing his eye with mine.

He grinned. "That's all right then – you're my favourite subject at the moment." His face turned serious and he returned my gaze intensely. "Can't stop thinking about you, actually."

I knew then that this would be all right. Difficult, yes. Harrowing for us both, probably. But the depth of that gaze and the warmth of his smile told me that it would be all right.

I took Josh through to the flat's open-plan living room with its panoramic view of virtually the whole of London laid out before us.

"Holy shit!" he exclaimed. "That's amazing. What a view!"

"Glad you like it," I said. "Being high on the hill is why I love this part of London so much. When I first came to view the place fifteen years ago, I got about as far as where you're standing now and just *knew*. I had to have it – far too expensive really, especially as I'd only just got my first job. But I've never regretted it."

"I bet you haven't! Wow, Steve, it's just awesome."

"Yes, I think it's kept me sane all these years – as sane as I am, that is. This view has kept me grounded and, I suppose, inspired me to keep going when it got tough."

"Why? I mean, why did you need to be inspired? And have you really been on your own all this time?" Again, that look in his eyes. Deep concern and care.

God, he's so adorable.

"Yep," I responded. "But we're going to get out of order if we start the story with this place. In many ways, this flat has been the culmination of my life so far."

We sat down on the sofa. It was a corner unit and I put Josh on the short edge so I was facing him. I needed to see him, to look him in the eye, whilst I told my story. There was a pause whilst I wondered where and how to begin.

"So were you born around here?" he asked.

"Good Lord, no. I'm a Yorkshireman by birth – I could have played cricket for them if I'd been any good! A small village in the Dales called Long Garfield was my home and bloody beautiful it was, too. True, the weather can get a bit shitty at times but I loved the place. Still do, I suppose, though I haven't been back for a long time, now."

"Are you still in touch with anybody there?"

"There's an aunt in the village – my mother's older sister, Auntie Meg. She's pushing eighty now but still as lively as ever. We talk once or twice a month usually. Her grandson Rob lives nearby, too." He smiled. "He got married last year to a big burly policeman called Owen. The village was flabbergasted but everybody was amazing and they had a fantastic party in the local pub."

I paused, realising that Josh's gentle questioning had

made me relax into my subject. Once more I was touched by this amazing man.

"So, go on then. What about school?"

"Junior school in the village. Three minutes' walk from home – I had a fabulous time for six years. Had a wonderful teacher, Miss Johnson. I did so love her when I was little." I grinned. "She's probably the only woman I've ever loved."

He laughed. "Apart from Barbara, of course."

"Oh, yes. Bless her. Anyway, I had lots of friends, then most of the kids moved on to secondary school in the local market town. I expected to do the same, but I won a scholarship to the local grammar school...'

I paused, remembering how exciting it was when we heard that I had got in to the grammar school. Mum and Dad had been so proud of me. We'd danced round the kitchen together after the letter had arrived. Then the reality dawned: leaving all my friends from junior school; travelling half an hour each way on the bus every day; not knowing how to behave with posh boys who would look down on a farm labourer's son. Finding the academic work intensive and difficult, at least at first.

A shadow must have crossed my face because Josh smiled gently and said, "Not so good, then, eh?"

"The first three years were difficult. The travelling was tedious and I missed my friends. I also found the work bloody hard whereas junior school had been a breeze."

"Yeah, I know what you mean," Josh replied. "The first and second forms at my secondary school were really tough as well. I began to think that I was really *thick*."

"Quite," I responded. "Then my life changed when a

scruffy little four-foot-nothing kid called Jamie started getting on the bus every day." My eyes filled when I mentioned his name and my throat constricted. Josh watched me intently and I saw his eyes widen as I paused. But I cleared my throat with a cough and carried on, bringing my voice under control.

"So, he was in the first form, two years younger than me, but somehow during those bus journeys we became friends. We had loads of interests in common – especially trains – and we liked the same music. As a result, we spent loads of time together outside school – trips to buy cassette or CD singles in Skipton on a Saturday afternoon, and hours on the bridge at our local station watching the railway."

"Sounds fun," said Josh. "I went trainspotting one summer because I had a crush on another boy who was really into it. I had a really good time."

I raised an eyebrow. "In more ways than one, I presume?"

"Well, we did have our moments. But then he decided he liked girls after all, so that was that." It was Josh's turn to look a little wistful but then he brightened and looked up at me again. "So did Jamie help you improve with your work?"

"And how. I don't know what it was really, but having Jamie as my friend made me feel special. I could do *anything* – all a matter of self-confidence, I suppose. So, by the time of my GCSEs, we knew that the bond between us was very deep. I was sixteen, he was fourteen, but he was the one who came out to me. He'd put on a growth spurt in the previous year so transformed from the four-foot-nothing kid I'd first met."

I paused again, struggling to keep control. Josh was still looking at me intently, eyes wide open, not knowing what to expect. It relaxed me for a moment so that I gave a short laugh. "He was now a feisty blond teenager who stood all of five foot five. He'd filled out a bit too – so... I just thought he was bloody gorgeous and I worshipped the ground he walked on."

I closed my eyes and took a series of deep breaths.

Josh spoke. "Take your time, Steve," he said. "Stop when you need to."

I smiled at him, and found the words to continue. "We had great times, those two years until I went to university. We came out to our parents, who were miraculously calm about the whole thing. Jamie insisted that we do it together to both sets of parents simultaneously. He was convinced that even if one of them was anti, they wouldn't dare say so in front of the others. I took a lot of stick over that from my mum. She'd known for ages, of course – as she said, you couldn't see Jamie and I together *without* knowing – but she was a bit offended that I hadn't felt able to confide in her."

"We had it all worked out, Jamie and I. I got a place at uni in Leeds, so we saw each other most weekends. He planned to apply to the same place and be with me for my final year. We could be together then and stay together – our forever moment, he called it. No civil partnerships or gay marriage in those days, of course."

"Quite," said Josh quietly.

I paused again, staring blankly into space. Trying to find the words to say the next bit.

The Year of Awakening

Chapter 17

Josh

I had lost him again. He stared at the coffee table, eyes unseeing. It was clear that we'd reached the nub of the story. It was going to end badly, that much was clear, and it was going to be awful because whatever it was had clearly ruined their relationship and pretty much the next twenty years of Steve's life. My heart ached for him and I so wanted to make it better for him. But for that to happen, I had to *know*.

I closed my eyes for a moment, willing myself to be patient and not to push him too hard. Then I heard a sharp intake of breath and Steve began to speak again. The words came out in a rapid-fire monotone, as if giving them no expression made them easier to say.

"Everything was going according to plan until the Christmas after my twenty-first birthday. It was the end of Jamie's first term at college. We were at home, staying with Jamie's parents. All of a sudden there was a bang on the door and there stood two policemen. Somebody had shopped us. They arrested me for having sex with Jamie when he was under the age of consent."

"Oh, my God! Steve! But surely— The law, it was changing?"

"Yes, they cut the age to eighteen the following year. But I later found out that I was one of 1,500 men who were prosecuted in that last year for the same offence, and one of the 500 found guilty. Quite a lot of us were sent to prison as well."

"Prison? Oh, fuck, Steve! They didn't!"

He nodded. "Two years, they sentenced me to. I'll never forget the look of sheer malice on the magistrate's face when he passed the sentence."

I was beginning to lose it. Watching the agony on Steve's face as he told me was difficult enough but then I began to imagine how he must have felt as all this had been going on. My emotions welled up and I let out a single sob. I'd been trying to remain calm for him but this was too much.

Steve held out his arms and I moved closer. He wrapped me in a hug, kissing me on the temple, and then resumed. "The worst part was sitting in the bloody police station being questioned about people I'd never even met or had anything to do with. They had convinced themselves that, because I was being charged with this one offence, I must be some form of predator who was going round corrupting the youth of the Dales. I was just a Yorkshire lad who was in a monogamous relationship with the love of my life. I wasn't a criminal or a monster but, by Christ, they made me feel like one. And then they knocked me about a bit because I wouldn't own up to any other offences. 'He's only a fucking queer,' one of them said. 'What's it matter?' Oh, God, Josh I was so fucking *terrified*."

I pushed closer to him on the sofa, as if trying to pass him strength through our skins. The tears started to roll down my face. The thought of all this happening to this loving and loved boy, ripping his life apart, was almost too much.

Steve spoke again, his voice trembling slightly. "I wasn't allowed to have any contact with Jamie during the run-up to the trial, but he supported me the best way he could via our parents. The last message I got from him was just after the trial. He would wait for me, he said, and I mustn't worry. Just get through it and we could resume our lives together. We'd still have our forever moment."

He paused again. And swallowed hard. "Two weeks later he was dead. Suicide, they said."

I sat up, absolutely horrified. Steve looked into my eyes with such an expression of pain and loss that I could hardly bear it. "He promised to wait for me, Josh. He was going to be there, he said. But he wasn't! Why didn't he wait?" His face crumpled and the tears welled up once more.

I'd had it. I drew Steve into a fierce hug and wept on his shoulder. At last he let go too, and the tension I had felt in his muscles drained away. His body was wracked with sobs; I could feel his tears on my neck.

Eventually, he became calm again and he relaxed even more into my arms. I realised that he had fallen asleep, exhausted by it all.

I lost track of time but I saw the sun set and watched as the view from the window changed into a spectacular show as the lights went on all over central London. It was a wonderful sight. My head ached appallingly but I tried to process all the information Steve had shared. I couldn't make any sense of it, though; every time I thought of the pair of them, so close for so long, being ripped apart and virtually destroyed, I wanted to cry again.

I nodded off myself for a few minutes, comforted by the warmth of the body I was still clamped to.

I awoke feeling a little better and my feelings had changed. I was still devastated by what Steve had told me but was also awed by the fact that he'd felt able to confide in me, of all people. I felt a terrific responsibility, now, to help him through all this and to encourage him to live the rest of his life in some sort of peace. My sentiments weren't entirely unselfish, of course; I recognised that our future together – if we were going to have one, and I *so* much wanted to have one – depended in large measure on Steve finding that peace.

Eventually, the figure in my arms stirred and I felt his lips brush my neck.

"Hey," I said. "Feeling better?" I felt rather than saw his head nod. "Good. And thank you."

Steve raised his head and looked at me questioningly. "What for?"

"For telling me your story. You trusted me enough to let yourself go. Unless I'm much mistaken, that was a bloody big step and I'm honoured."

He smiled. "That's a nice thing to say, Josh. Thanks. And thank you for listening. I have to tell you about prison, though, before we're done."

"God, Steve. Was it awful?"

He nodded and I saw his eyes fill once more. He sighed and spoke in a monotone again. "I survived. I managed to latch on to one of the gang bosses in there and became his bitch. It saved me from the attentions of others and he wasn't a bad sort in some ways. He never wanted to use me for anything other than somewhere to put his dick. I wasn't required to kiss him or even get off myself, I just had to be available for him to fuck whenever he wanted. I managed to cope with that because somehow it became just a bodily function like any other. My mind wasn't involved at all. It was something I had to do to survive. I got through it – I even got out early for extra good behaviour.

"After my release, I came straight to a hostel in London and began the process of changing my name by deed poll. I couldn't face going back to the village. My parents had moved away and were living in Devon. Jamie's parents emigrated to Australia to try to start again. I kept in touch with Auntie Meg and she came down here to see me several times, latterly accompanied by her grandson. That's how I got to know Rob, though I've never met Owen.

"I never went back to uni. I got an Open University degree and switched to Environmental Studies – which is how I came to found Pearson Frazer with Andy and Barbara."

"Gosh, Steve," I breathed. "How on earth did you manage that all on your own?"

"The short answer is with great difficulty. What made it worse was the fact that I'd never been on my own before. My family had always been very close and then Jamie was part of my life, as friend or lover, from the age of fourteen. I didn't know what loneliness was until I went to prison."

I hugged him tighter again, once more groping for words to express how his story made me feel.

However, Steve spoke first. "That was why this flat came

to be so important to me after I found it fifteen years ago. It was my sanctuary, somewhere I could feel safe no matter what shit was happening to me elsewhere. If I couldn't face work or any other type of activity, I could sit and stare at that view. It was never boring, it was always changing, and I knew that it would eventually make me feel better." He gave a short bark of laughter. "So you can imagine how many hours I've wasted sitting here staring into space."

"Well, it is really something else. I can see how you could become attached to it."

Steve nodded. "I suppose I was trying to build a new identity that had nothing to do with the boy I was in Jamie's time. I needed to construct the hard shell round myself that would hold me together." He paused and grinned at me. "You know, the shell that was so tough that you smashed it within three minutes of walking into my office for an interview."

Chapter 18

Steve

Josh looked away and blushed slightly but then looked up, eyes wide and questioning. "Gosh! Steve, does that mean... I mean *instantly*? Christ!"

I laughed, "Yes, I fell for you straight away, Josh Ashcroft. Which of course was why my defences went up. There was no way that I wanted you anywhere near the firm, because I was frightened of what it would unleash. And perhaps you understand why after this afternoon."

He nodded solemnly. "I can see that, absolutely. Undermining the life you thought you'd built up and tearing through your defences. Poor you. You must have been terrified."

"Oh, and there's one other thing you should know," I added, twisting my mouth into a sardonic smile. "You are the first person I have kissed properly since I last kissed Jamie two minutes before the police arrived twenty-one years ago."

"Christ," he breathed. "Steve, that is so awesome. Why? I mean, why me? I... I feel... God! What a responsibility! I bet that would even have floored Rhett Butler."

His deflection into humour was classic Josh and one of the many things that endeared him to me. I laughed and then grinned at him wolfishly. "Which means, of course, that I've got a lot of wasted time to make up."

His stomach chose that moment to rumble, protesting at the lack of any recent food. I laughed again. "Oh yes, I seem to remember promising to feed you as well. I'd better go and put the lasagne in the oven."

Josh was suitably impressed by my culinary skills and we spent the evening joking, washing the pasta down with a nice bottle of Italian red. I felt almost light-headed with relief that I had managed to find the words that afternoon. I had never told the full story before to a living soul. Barbara knew the rough outline but I had never told her about the prison bit, and never really acknowledged just how important Jamie had been to me. She had probably worked that out for herself but I had always shied away from talking about him – as if I were frightened of making my sense of loss even more tangible, even after more than twenty years.

Josh was amazing – supportive, sympathetic and so kind. No judgements. I was so grateful and the whole business served to deepen my feelings for him. I looked up at him now to find him grinning at me.

"Were they pretty?" he asked.

I shook my head. "Er – what?"

"Well, you've obviously been away with the fairies for the last five minutes, so I wondered whether they were pretty."

I laughed. "Sometimes you have a mind like a cryptic

crossword. Yes, the subject of my thoughts is very pretty indeed, since I was actually thinking about you."

Josh blushed and swallowed hard. Then he looked at me and blinked. He was irresistible.

I moved from the dining table towards the sofa, holding my hand out to beckon him to join me. "Come on, and I'll tell you all about my wicked thoughts."

He entwined his fingers with mine and joined me on the sofa, tucking himself into my side and resting his head on my shoulder.

"I was thinking about how marvellous you were this afternoon, helping me deal with my past," I told him. "I was terrified that it would freak you out and send you running."

"Ha! You don't get rid of me that easily. Seriously, though, I think you're so brave – I can imagine how difficult it was – and I'm so relieved that you could actually get the words out. I was thinking while you were asleep that whatever we might have together is about the future but we have to let go of the past in order to enjoy it, I think... God, I'm burbling. Sorry."

"No, you're not," I responded. "You're absolutely right. I've spent all these years running away from the future because I had no hope that it could be better than the past. You've given me that hope."

Josh twisted in my embrace and brought his lips to mine with a feather-light touch. "You say the nicest things to me, Scarlett," he murmured. I returned the kiss, which suddenly took on a different character. It was urgent and passionate – Josh tasted of our dessert and his lips were soft and yielding. Holding him close to me with my arm wrapped around his waist felt so bloody beautiful. God, how I had missed all this!

After a few minutes, he lifted himself so that he straddled me and our erections brushed against each other, increasing the passion and urgency of our kisses.

"Come to bed," I said.

"Oh yes, please," he replied. "I thought you'd never ask."

As we moved into my bedroom, the feelings of relief and lightness that I'd begun to experience after telling my story were replaced by nerves. A heaviness formed in my stomach and I wondered what would happen next. This was so important to me and I so wanted everything to go well. But I hadn't done anything like this for such a long time, so I was bound to muck it up the first time. I began to shake slightly and hesitated on the threshold of my bedroom.

Suddenly I felt Josh's hand in the small of my back, rubbing lightly. "Hey," he whispered. "It'll be okay. Don't overthink this. It's been a long time for me too…"

God, this boy was incredible!

We helped each other out of our clothes, pausing for a gentle caress or two and light kisses. When we were undressed except for our underwear, we joined in a full embrace. The feeling of another man almost naked in my arms was incredible – my breathing became ragged with the sheer sensation of it, and once again Josh moved to calm me.

He moved me over to the bed and we lay down side by side, shedding our boxers and kissing gently.

"God, I've wanted this for so long!" I breathed. "Just to

hold somebody else."

Josh grinned at me. "Yes, pretty good, eh? Me, I've dreamed about kissing you ever since that day we had the row. For two pins, I'd have done it there and then, but I thought your reaction might be a little hostile."

"It might well have been," I smiled back.

He moved in for another kiss and reached round to the back of my head to release the band that held my ponytail in place.

"That's something else I've dreamt of doing," he said, looking at me intently. "Losing myself in your hair, seeing it splayed out on the pillow around you." He combed his hand through my hair, spreading it out. "Steve, you're so beautiful."

We kissed again, this time more passionately than ever, and Josh rolled on top of me. He reached between us to adjust the position of our cocks.

"Careful, Josh," I whispered. "It wouldn't take much."

"No, me neither. Let's just go with the flow, shall we?"

I nodded.

In response, he moved his body so that it rippled across mine. Then he began to thrust with his hips and a host of new sensations took over. I matched his movements and the friction this generated, together with the heat of our bodies, was so arousing as we moved together. I knew I wasn't going to last long.

Josh fixed me with another passionate kiss and broke it to say, "Christ, Steve, gonna come!"

This was enough to push me over the edge as well. The orgasm swept through my whole body, causing an involuntary spasm in my limbs as I shouted his name.

Moments later, Josh too went over the edge and I felt his body shake in my arms as he let out a cry.

We lay together in the same position for a few moments as we came down from our several highs and recovered our breath. Suddenly, he raised himself and looked down into my eyes. He grinned. "Gosh, Mr Frazer, that was jolly nice."

"Thank you, Mr Ashcroft. I thought it was bloody marvellous."

"But things down there are a bit messy now."

"Yes. How would you like to shower with me?"

"I think I would like that very much."

Chapter 19

Josh

Fortunately, Steve had a capacious shower cubicle in his en suite but, even so, it was difficult not to keep touching each other. After a few moments, he grabbed the shower gel and began to wash my body. His movements were slow and sensuous and I found myself waking up down below despite the intensity of my recent orgasm.

He washed me with care and attention and those few minutes were some of the most sensuous and erotic I had ever experienced. When he finished, he kissed me again, but so gently and carefully that I moaned into his mouth. I returned the compliment, washing his body first and then shampooing all that wonderful hair, losing myself in the joy of massaging his scalp. By this time, the water was starting to cool so Steve turned the shower off and passed me a towel.

We had hardly spoken, losing ourselves in the sensuality of the moment. I felt as if I ought to break the silence but couldn't think of anything to say.

He was bent over drying my leg and smiled up at me.

"You okay?"

"More than."

"Need anything? Drink or something?"

"Just the tap water is fine."

He headed back to the bed, glancing back at me over his shoulder with a slightly hesitant look. "You will stay? Please?"

I smiled. "Of course, Scarlett. Who could resist such a sexy man?"

"Oh, Rhett, you do say the nicest things."

Once in bed, we entwined our legs and settled into a close embrace.

"That's nice," I said. "We fit together rather nicely. I'm definitely a cuddly sort of person."

He laughed gently. "Idiot. Anyway, I should be the judge of whether you're cuddly or not."

"Fair enough," I giggled. "So what's the verdict?"

"Satisfactory, I think," then he grinned. "But there does seem to be something a bit stiff in the way."

"Really?"

"Yes, maybe we should deal with that and then I'll give you my verdict on your cuddliness."

"Sounds like a plan," I replied, moving in for a kiss. I closed my eyes – I could lose myself with the sensation of those lips for ever. The smell of Steve's shower gel and shampoo was intoxicating and the feel of his hands moving over my back and hips was almost too erotic. When his hands moved downwards and began to squeeze my arse, I knew what I wanted.

"Steve, will you top me, please?"

"Are you sure?" he asked gently.

"Yes, I've never been so sure of anything in my life. I need to feel you inside me, to make the connection."

Steve's brow furrowed for a moment and he looked uncertain, biting his bottom lip and looking like a small boy puzzling over a problem.

"Hey, it's okay," I said, "if you'd rather not. I'm sorry if...'

He cut me off. "No, no, that's not the point. It's just that ... it's stupid really ... but I've never done that before. Jamie and I didn't ever get to that... I've never fucked a man – anybody come that. A bit of admission, eh?" He let out a short bark of laughter. "Got to age forty-two and never 'done it'."

"What you have or haven't done in the past is irrelevant, Steve. It's what you want to do *now* that matters. And I must say that I'd be really delighted to be your first – in fact I bloody love the idea. We'll take it slowly and if you feel uncomfortable at any point, you must say so and we'll stop."

He said nothing for a moment but kissed me gently. Then he spoke. "Thanks, Josh, I'd like that. And I do have supplies."

I grinned. "Did you buy them in hope or expectation?"

He blushed and looked like a little boy again. I kissed the end of his nose. "I know, you were a Boy Scout, and follow the motto 'Be Prepared'."

"Oh, I am always prepared for anything," he responded. He reached across me to his bedside table. He extracted some lube and a packet of condoms and placed them on the bed.

He flipped us over in the bed so that he was on top of

me, then began to move down my body leaving a trail of feather-light kisses before biting my nipples. I arched into his touch – he felt so warm. When he arrived at my crotch, he looked up at me intently before taking my cock into his mouth.

"Oh, God," I cried. "That feels sensational."

His hands continued their explanation and I spread my legs to allow him better access. I felt his finger exploring between my arse cheeks. He found the hole and circled round it gently. He withdrew for a moment and I felt the chill of the lube on his finger entering me. I made a conscious effort to relax and enjoy the feeling of penetration. I lifted my legs further.

"More," I said. "Please."

He added a second finger, working both in and out. The sensation was wonderful, and it had been so long...

His fingers withdrew and I immediately missed them. There was a rustle of the condom packet followed by more lube. Then he was back, pushing gently to penetrate me. As he slipped past the first ring, I felt the burn of being fully stretched. He stayed still for a moment or two, breathing heavily, hair hanging in front of his eyes like a curtain. Then he moved further in, barely a millimetre at a time, until he was fully home.

"Josh," he breathed. "What a feeling. So tight! So beautiful. God, I'm not going to last long."

"Just relax and enjoy," I responded. "It's okay now, you can move."

He shifted and began a series of short, tentative thrusts, which became deeper as he gained confidence. He picked up a steady rhythm and kept up a steady flow of murmurs and expletives. He was lost in the joy of the moment. I revelled in the feeling of fullness and the deep connection between us – every nerve end was sensitised and I knew that my orgasm was not far away.

I reached for my own cock, but Steve swatted my hand away and gripped it himself, rubbing me in sync with his own thrusts. I reached up and brushed his hair to one side. His eyes, which had been closed, opened in response to my touch. He looked into my eyes, and I felt the connection between us so strongly. The moment passed as the first wave of my orgasm hit me, quickly followed by his. He thrust deep and cried out. He collapsed on top of me and kissed me long and hard.

He moved off after a couple of minutes and disappeared into the bathroom for a few moments, returning with a warm damp facecloth to clean me down. He did this with as much care as he had washed me earlier in the shower, and then towelled me dry. He came back to bed and scooted across to take me in his arms once more.

We had not spoken but the silence between us was comfortable rather than awkward. I felt safe in his arms and snuggled even closer.

"Mmm," he said. "You feel so nice, folded in there. Purpose built, I'd say, wouldn't you?"

"Spot on," I said. "So did I pass the cuddliness test?"

"With flying colours, my boy, with flying colours."

"Steve, I feel...'

But he placed his finger on my lips and smiled down at me. "Shh, Josh. No declarations tonight, all right? Time for sleep."

So saying, he kissed my temple and settled himself

down, dropping off almost immediately. I lay there and watched him sleep for a few minutes, thinking of all that had happened today and all the pain he had endured. Once more a tear leaked from my eye until I too fell into a deep sleep.

Chapter 20

Steve

It was just getting light when I awoke in urgent need of the bathroom. I extricated myself from Josh's arms as gently as possible and he didn't stir. Even so, he was awake when I returned to bed and opened one eye to look at me.

"Hey there, little one," I breathed. "Sorry to wake you. It's only five, so we should go back to sleep. We had a heavy day yesterday."

"S'okay," he responded sleepily. "Need to go myself, really."

I curled up on my side under the blanket awaiting his return, so that when he joined me again, he lay against my back. "Hmm, that feels nice," he said.

As he moved, I felt his erection brush my backside and lodge between my cheeks. I felt my body stiffen involuntarily, ready to resist the invasion. God, where had that come from? Clearly, there were some things that time had yet to heal.

Josh sensed the shift immediately and moved away. "Sorry, I should have thought. Some things you're not ready for."

I turned over to face him and kissed him on the end of his nose. "Don't apologise. I didn't see that coming at all – purely instinctive."

We lay there quietly. I was just enjoying holding this incredible man and it made me smile contentedly. Josh's breathing became regular once more. He'd drifted back to sleep again and I thought I should do the same. A few minutes later, I did.

When I awoke, I was in bed alone. I could hear the noise of the shower next door. Suddenly a voice began to sing and I realised it was Josh. It was a rich baritone sound and I lay in bed captivated as he sang 'Luck Be A Lady' from *Guys and Dolls* – clearly still a favourite from the days of his school production. Then he shifted into 'I'll Know When My Love Comes Along,' which finished as he turned off the shower. He was seriously talented and I was seriously impressed.

At that moment he emerged from the bathroom with a towel wrapped round his waist, curly hair all over the place. He noticed that I was awake, made the connection with his singing and immediately blushed.

"Did I wake you with my caterwauling? I'm really sorry – it's a bad habit of mine to sing in the bathroom. I never thought."

"No, don't worry. I was already awake when you started. You have a very beautiful voice, young Rhett."

"Why thank you, kind sir. Yeah, it's okay – never quite

good enough, though, I'm afraid."

"What do you mean? Who said?"

"All sorts of people. It's a long story and I'm too hungry to bother with it now. I was going to make you breakfast in bed. Is that okay? How does French toast sound?"

I felt that I had been brushed off over the singing, but I would come back to the subject later on. Meanwhile, the idea of staying in bed and being fed my breakfast on a platter was rather appealing.

"French toast sounds divine. And thanks. Breakfast in bed is a wonderful idea." I grinned. "But what are you going to feed me after that?"

"Ah, well, we'll just have to wait and see," he responded, cocking an eyebrow.

Josh's bedroom treats included breakfast – with French toast, orange juice and coffee – and then the opportunity to taste various parts of his anatomy, which we both found very rewarding. Afterwards I showed him the rest of the flat, including my office/study, where he espied my electronic keyboard. I'd bought it the previous year as part of a resolution to broaden my horizons. I had enjoyed playing the piano as a boy but any sustained interest as an adult had been fractured by my imprisonment and its consequences.

Josh was enthusiastic. "I haven't seen anything as nice as that for a long time," he exclaimed, brushing his fingers across the keys. "Mind if I have a go? I haven't played anything since I was at home last at Christmas," he added.

"Be my guest," I responded. I leant across him and flicked the on switch, kissing the top of his head. "If you're half as good as you were singing in the shower, I'm in for a treat."

He blushed slightly and made a sound which sounded a bit like the modern equivalent of 'phsaw.'

He limbered up with a few scales, played in a manner which indicated a high degree of skill. Then he struck up a song, one I immediately recognised but couldn't put a name to. He reminded me later that it was Gershwin, called 'Someone to Watch Over Me.' After a straight rendition of the tune, he launched into a jazz version with variations in and out of the main theme that I am sure was worthy of greats like Oscar Peterson or – my own favourite – George Shearing. He finished his performance with a perfect rendition of the lyrics, once more in a fine, rich, baritone voice.

I stood there open mouthed. When he finished, I clapped my hands and patted him on the shoulder. "Fantastic," I told him. "Thanks so much."

He smiled briefly and reached for the off switch. "Thanks for letting me have a go. It's a lovely instrument."

"You're welcome to come and play it any time," I responded, adding with a grin, "so long as you play tunes on my body afterwards."

He groaned at the cheesy joke. "Right, come on – I need some fresh air. How about a quick trot around the park?"

It was my turn to groan at the thought of all that exercise on top of our other exertions the previous night and most of this morning. On the other hand, the sun had come out after a wet start and it seemed too good an opportunity to miss. Daylight saving time had not yet started, so the sun was already quite low in the sky, bathing the houses and the park in a form of luminous low relief.

"What a glorious afternoon," I exclaimed as we entered Paxton's park, designed and built to surround his Crystal Palace. The palace itself might have been destroyed but the park – including its famous collection of prehistoric monsters – had survived and prospered. It was one of my favourite places and it looked great in the sharp light of the late winter afternoon. We jogged down the main avenue, round the lake and up past the athletics stadium. We doubled back to the café and sat drinking coffee.

"I love to imagine the elegant ladies in their crinolines parading up and down this path under their parasols," I said.

"Or the swells in their top hats. All dark eyes and sweeping moustaches," Josh laughed. I loved the way the skin either side of his eyes crinkled when he was amused by something – which seemed to be quite often. But I was also conscious of his ability to use humour to deflect conversations away from what he felt to be dangerous ground. He'd done this several times when his performing career was mentioned; there was something there to be unlocked. I was no professional by any means, but I could recognise talent when I saw it and Josh had it in bucket loads. So what had gone wrong? He had mentioned issues of stage fright the other week when we were in Bristol. Where had that come from?

Something told me that the desire to play, sing and perform was central to Josh's being. An event, or possibly a person, had made him lock the door on it and try to hide the key. Instinctively I knew that I had to unlock that door again if I was going to know the real Josh. All this came to me in a flash; it takes far longer to describe the feelings and the processes that were going through my brain than the few seconds it took me to reach this conclusion. The question was, though, how to unlock the door.

I spoke and the way he jumped suggested that he'd gone into a reverie too. "So, if dashing young men in top hats is your dream of the past, what's your dream of the future?"

He grinned at me. "That's easy: it's getting to know a clever environmental consultant who's going to be so famous that I'll never need to work again. He'll keep me in the style to which I wish to become accustomed."

"Oh, so your ambition is to become a kept man, is it?"

"Absolutely." He laughed before narrowing his eyes and looking straight into mine. "Provided you're the one doing the keeping."

I confess to having been a little thrown by that and I missed a beat or two before replying. I returned his steady gaze. "Oh, I'm a keeper, Joshua Ashcroft. Have no doubt of that."

I realised that he'd done it again, deflected me from my original question. "So imagine you were a kept man, what would you do all day? Play your piano?"

"Oh, eat chocolates and drink champagne, I think, whilst reading romantic novels about..."

"Don't tell me, let me guess, environmental consultants who become successful and fall in love with their staff."

He laughed at that. "Something like that. Only I'm too busy living the dream to write it all down."

"Living the dream, eh? Falling in love and settling down.

Bet that wasn't your dream when you were eighteen."

"Oh, no, then I was going to be Larry Olivier and Fred Astaire all rolled into one superstar!"

"So what happened, Josh?" I asked gently, reaching for his hand.

He took my hand and entwined his fingers with mine as a deep shadow passed over his face. "Greg happened. That's what."

"Do you want to talk about it?"

"Not really, no," he replied in a flat tone. "But I know I must, just as you had to tell me about Jamie."

"That bad, eh?" I asked gently.

"Compared with your experience, a walk in the park," he replied, smiling sadly and gesturing around us. "But it was tough, and I don't think I'm fully over it yet."

He shivered. I looked up and noticed that the sun was slipping below the horizon. "You're getting cold," I said. "Come on, let's get you home in the warm and then I can cuddle you better."

He grinned, losing the air of melancholy that had descended over him in the last few minutes. "Now that sounds like a *seriously* good idea. Last one back has to do the washing up." So saying, he set off back to the flat at a brisk pace.

The Year of Awakening

Chapter 21

Josh

I had known all weekend that I would have to tell my story too, and I'd been trying to put it off; this weekend had been about Steve and I didn't want my melancholy little drama intruding on to his healing process. On the other hand, he had to know and understand my past if we were going to have a future together.

So it was that, having got back to the flat, showered and changed, we were once more installed on Steve's sofa, arms wrapped round each other.

"So, tell me about Greg," Steve commanded gently.

"I think I told you that I went to drama school aged eighteen, straight from secondary school. I was out and proud, as they say, but still incredibly naïve and a bit gauche. Oh, I could play a smooth and sophisticated guy like Sky Masterson, but the aura was only skin deep – it was only a character I was playing, not the real me. Greg was in his final year at the same drama school. He was actually a mature student, so was eight years older than me.

"To cut a long story short, I fell for him – hook, line and sinker. He was my 'forever' man and showed every sign of reciprocating. We moved in together at the end of my first term. And then began the long, steady process of undermining my confidence until he totally controlled me. Effectively, I was his slave."

Steve gasped involuntarily but I patted his arm in reassurance. "Oh, not in any kinky way. He wasn't into bondage or S&M or anything like that. No, he just took over my life. When we first moved in together, for instance, we shared the domestic tasks. Gradually, the burden shifted to me. I was only a student whereas he was now a jobbing actor and making quite a good living out of it. So his career came first, because that was what was feeding us. Towards the end of my first year, he tried to persuade me that it would be a good idea for me to take a year out of the course so that I could look after him full time while his career developed. When I baulked at the idea, the abuse started. Not physical or anything like that, just the drip, drip of negative remarks and criticisms, whittling away at my self-confidence all the time.

"I had secured quite a big part in the end-of-term production in my first year – I was to be Simon, the son in *Hay Fever*. There was quite a lot to learn but Greg wouldn't help. Said playing Coward's comedy was too much for me, I was working too hard, and questioned whether this was the career for me. He said he loved me and wanted to look after me and didn't like me getting stressed."

Steve tightened his arm round my shoulders. The recollections were certainly stressing me – I suddenly realised that my body was rigid with tension. I was tempted to stop, to tell him that I couldn't go on, that he didn't need to know any of this. But that would have been untrue. He needed – and obviously wanted – to know. I forced myself to relax and resumed the story.

"End-of-term plays at drama schools are pretty big occasions, especially here in London. The big agents, casting directors from film and TV, the theatre companies, they're all there. They're talent spotting so it's a terrific opportunity for the kids who get cast." I laughed. "You tend to get the *most* committed performances, even from the second spear carrier."

Steve laughed too, and this helped release some of my tension – but it quickly returned as I resumed my narrative.

"To cut a long story short," I said, "I froze on the first night and completely lost it. It was during the second act, the party scene. I don't know whether you know the play, but Simon and his sister have a row over a game they and their guests are playing after dinner. I can see it now. I was enjoying the interaction with the girl who was playing Sorrel, then something just clicked in my brain. One moment I knew the next line, where I was and so forth, and the next moment I didn't. I just froze and gaped at the audience. Then I passed out." I could feel the sting of unshed tears in my eyes. "I've not been on a stage since."

"Josh!"

I gave him a wan smile. He squeezed my hand and I carried on. "That night, Greg took me home and looked after me, but of course it was the worst thing that could have happened. He had me drop out of school to reduce my stress levels and, because by then pretty much everything got me stressed, I did nothing at all. I stopped going out.

'Stay safe,' he said. My only activity was to keep the flat nice and clean for him. To pay him back for all his care, he said.

"For several months, I cooked and cleaned and washed and ironed for him, but of course it was never quite good enough. There was always some criticism, something not quite right, a way that it could be improved next time if only I listened to Greg."

"Josh, what on earth happened? How did you get out of it?"

"My friend Robbie – you know, the one I share the house with now. He was worried about me. He'd been in the audience that night and since then he hadn't seen me for months. We'd been at secondary school together and then gone to the same drama school. We very close in our first term before I met Greg, but he'd quickly been excluded after that."

"He came round to see me one Saturday but Greg refused to let him in. He said I wasn't well. For some reason, Robbie smelt a rat and he came back during the day on the Monday, waited till he knew I was on my own. He stayed for about an hour but deliberately didn't say much. He told me later that he realised what was going on and was really worried, so he rang my parents. They turned up the next morning and more or less frog-marched me out of the flat."

"My God, Josh. How did you feel about that?"

I smiled. "Funnily enough, the penny dropped when Robbie told me on the Monday that Greg had refused to let him in. He'd lied to him. I knew then that I had to get out but knowing and working out how to do it were two different things, you know?"

"Oh, yes, I can understand that. Prevaricating is the easiest thing in the world."

"The really odd thing was that as soon as I got home, I felt such a fool. Why had I not realised it earlier? Was I so stupid that I had allowed everything I'd ever dreamed of to be destroyed just for the sake of what I thought of as love? I was so *angry*."

"Yeah, but you didn't do anything wrong, did you? You loved somebody and he betrayed you by abusing you mentally – seeking to control you for his own purposes. The blame lies solely with him, Josh. Surely you must see that?"

I gave a short laugh. "You're certainly not the first person to have told me that. Robbie, my parents, my doctor, my therapist... They've all spent the last eight years trying to get me to stop blaming myself. Don't get me wrong, I can see the argument and it's entirely logical. Absolutely. But somewhere deep down in here..." I tapped my chest "...I curse my own stupidity. Then there's the other little voice that says he was right and my talent was not good enough; that his advice to give it all up and play safe was the best thing for me."

I stared blankly ahead for a few moments then looked up and smiled crookedly. "And of course you can bet that little voice pipes up every time I even think about going back to the stage, even as an amateur. That's why I was so stressed the other day in Bristol. You have no idea how much it meant to me, getting through that meeting and even coming to enjoy it."

Steve hugged me even closer and kissed my temple. The

gesture melted my heart.

"Well, as long as I'm around, that little voice will get a good telling off every time it speaks."

I grinned. "Oh, Scarlett, you do say the sweetest things to little ol' me!" I dropped the humour again quickly, though, and drove all the flightiness from my voice. "Seriously, thanks for listening to all that shit. It always helps to talk about it." I snorted gently. "We're a right pair, aren't we?"

"Yes, I suppose we are. But you know what they say: 'United we stand, div—'"

Steve's utterance remained incomplete as I leaned towards him and planted a kiss on his lips. All conversation was suspended.

"What's the plan for this week? You're away for a couple of nights, aren't you?" I asked. We had made love again after my confession then Steve had made some supper. It was getting late and we hadn't really talked about where things went from here.

"Yeah," he replied. "Tuesday and Wednesday – and I probably won't get back till late on Thursday. I've got two long meetings and then I'm speaking at a conference in Manchester." He grinned. "More flag waving for Pearson Frazer."

"Sounds like a tough week," I responded.

"Especially as I haven't written my speech yet. That was pencilled in for this weekend, but something else came up and I've been a bit … er… distracted."

"Oh, really?" I replied with a grin, reaching across to stroke his thigh. "I can't think what that was."

"No, I bet you can't, especially as you're now doing it again."

"Me? Doing what?" I moved my hand up his leg, stroking him with a gentle circular motion.

"That, you sod! Stroking me like that is certainly going to get both of us into trouble."

I laughed and withdrew my hand. He pouted and grinned at me.

"Sounds as if I should head homewards, so that I can be all bright-eyed and bushy-tailed for my sexy boss in the morning."

"I'd love you to stay, but…" Steve looked a little sad for a moment but then he brightened. "Are you free next weekend?"

I nodded enthusiastically. "Try and keep me away."

"Right, dinner Friday night. I'll pick you up around seven. Oh, and if it's okay with you, I plan to tell Andy and Barbara that we're dating. I don't want to hide anything from them and I'm sure it'll be easier if they know."

"Gosh!" I replied, swallowing hard. "Are you sure? Not about us dating but about telling them?"

"Would you rather I didn't?" Steve responded, giving me a questioning look.

"No, no. I think it's very sensible. I was just taken aback a little, I suppose." I grinned at him. "Does that mean I can claim you as my *boyfriend*?"

"Do you want to be? Publicly tied up with an old wreck like me?"

"Steve, you mustn't say that, even in jest. I would be

139

proud to be your boyfriend." I paused, suddenly needing to say more. "In fact, I would be happy to be called anything so long as I can be close to you and hold you in my arms." I paused and added quickly, "Sorry that was a bit OTT, I think."

Steve's eyes opened wide and I was sure I spotted the glistening of a tear in the corner of his eye. "Not at all, Josh, it was a lovely thing to say." He hugged me and kissed the end of my nose. "Now go home before I do something really naughty with you."

Chapter 22

Steve

The flat certainly seemed empty without Josh. It was late and I should have gone to bed, but I pottered round tidying up, reluctant for the day to end. Eventually I succumbed to temptation and poured myself another glass of wine. I went to my favourite chair and sat down to stare out over the lights of London.

It was difficult to accept that it was only twenty-nine hours or so since Josh had arrived the previous afternoon, looking so sexy in his tight tee shirt and jeans. Excerpts from our conversion kept flashing through my mind. His reaction to all the shit I had thrown at him was all I could have asked for – kind, compassionate and non-judgemental. I could still feel the warmth of his body in my arms on the sofa as I told my story. I knew how much I had missed that human contact for the last twenty years.

Looking back now, I felt more serene about the past than ever before. Telling the story had no doubt been cathartic in itself, but I realised that could never have worked on its own; it would never have been enough. Telling Josh helped so much because I had such strong feelings for him.

That thought had me sitting up at attention in my chair. Well, I might as well accept it and relax into the sensations it brought. I was falling in love with Josh – and as I'd said to him the previous day, Pandora's box had been opened. There was no getting everything back in and battened down. For the last few weeks, the thought of loving Josh had caused me to panic, to want to run away and hide.

Tonight, though, there was no panic. The last few hours had proved to me that I could more than cope with loving Josh. I could face the consequences, whatever they may be. As I drained my glass and headed for the bedroom, I felt happier and more contented than at any time since my arrest, twenty-one years earlier. It was a novel sensation, a feeling that I was not going to give up lightly.

I got ready for bed and was about to climb in when my phone pinged. It was a text from Josh.

JOSH: >> Hey, Scarlett, you in bed yet?

STEVE:>> Just about to climb aboard. Wish you were here to tuck me in though, Rhett.

JOSH:>> Missing me already, eh? Nice... But I know what you mean. Missing you too. See you in the morning.

>STEVE: Yeah. Sleep tight.

The texts were inconsequential and silly but they made me smile and confirmed my feeling of contentment. I lay down and fell asleep almost immediately.

I arrived in the office early on Monday morning and was first in. Barbara and Andy were also early arrivals, which suited me fine. It meant that I could haul them into my office and say what I had to say without raising any eyebrows.

"Sorry to interrupt first thing but I wanted to tell you both that, as of last night, Josh and I have declared ourselves to be boyfriends."

As I might have predicted, Barbara leapt up from her chair and I found myself enveloped in a big hug. "Darling Steve," she said, "I am so pleased."

I grinned at her. "I thought you might be since you virtually threw me into his arms last week."

Andy laughed. "From where I was sitting, you didn't need to be thrown. It was pretty obvious you were smitten."

"No, I certainly didn't throw him," replied Barbara, joining in the laughter. "He only needed a little shove."

"Anyway, whatever," I said. "I just wanted you to know, to save any embarrassment."

"What about the rest of the staff? Shouldn't they know too?" asked Andy.

"Well, yeah, though I'm not keen on the idea of standing up and making a big announcement. Apart from anything else, it would freak poor Josh out, being the centre of attention like that."

Barbara smiled. "There's no need for any of that. I'll just let it be known to somebody. That'll ensure it's all round the building in no time. I bet they'll all be as pleased we are."

The Year of Awakening

Chapter 23

Josh

Though Steve had warned me of his plan to tell Andy and Barbara, I was not prepared for the intensity of their reaction, particularly Barbara's. She had me in a big hug within two minutes of walking into the building on Monday morning and I got a very warm handshake and pat on the back from Andy. I was very touched.

The week passed in a haze of good wishes from the other staff members and the atmosphere around the whole office was buoyant. The trouble came after work: though we had only been together for the one weekend, I missed Steve terribly.

At first I couldn't think why it hurt so much. I wandered round the house on the Monday evening, unable to settle to anything. Fortunately, both Robbie and Malcolm were out, so I didn't drive them mad with my constant fidgeting. Eventually I calmed down sufficiently to go to sleep after Steve and I spent ten minutes exchanging silly text messages just before bedtime.

Tuesday night was even worse to start with. The fact that

Steve was two hundred and more miles away in Manchester, rather than in his flat round the corner writing a speech, made it seem worse. When I welled up for the third time, I gave myself a good talking to and calmed down. The feeling of emptiness was probably the result of the intensity of the emotions we had shared.

For both of us, telling our stories was a moment akin to coming out. Neither of us had ever spoken of our feelings and reactions to another living soul and the process of doing so had drawn us very close.

Steve's absence did, however, give me the opportunity to do some serious thinking about the future. The fact that I had been able to play and sing for Steve over the weekend had meant a huge amount. Even though I had waved aside his compliments about my talents, they really did mean a lot to me. Nobody had said anything so nice to me for a long time. And then there was the feeling of using my voice in that way for the first time in more than four years – it had been exciting and liberating.

Could I have a future in performing? That was what I needed, even if I kept my day job and only did the occasional am-dram production or an open-mike night in a pub. It was the adrenaline rush of connecting with an audience that I craved again.

The first time these thoughts occurred to me on the Monday night, part of my brain pushed them away. Of course it was a silly idea – why subject yourself to such unnecessary stress? Look what had happened in *Hay Fever*: did I really want – could I really handle – another meltdown like that? Of course not.

And yet...

By Tuesday night, the doubts were starting to subside. I recognised Greg's voice in the 'do nothing' advice, which made me even more determined to do the opposite. I had joked to Steve about being Larry Olivier and Fred Astaire rolled into one – but the intent that lay beneath that joke was there. My performance as Sky Masterson all those years ago had shown me what it could be like: the exhilaration of the singing, the feeling of getting lost in the character, the thrill of the dance sequence and then the salute to the audience. Yes, it was only a school show, and of course they were going to go wild, but the thrill of it had stayed with me all this time. What a fool I had been to let Greg take that all from me.

By Wednesday evening, I was pacing up and down my flat trying to work out what I would need to do to get back to performance standards. It would involve a great deal of very hard work. Steve might have praised my little show on Sunday, but that had been one song imperfectly remembered and not very well played. To perform in public, even at an open-mike night, I'd need to have a repertoire that I knew backwards, a singing technique I'd perfected and an ability to accompany myself on a keyboard. That would require serious amounts of time and effort – and a keyboard. I couldn't afford one of my own at present – and then the idea occurred to me. Could I borrow Steve's? I had no doubt that his invitation to play as often as I wanted had been genuine – but could he put up with all the hard work and repetition that level of rehearsal would entail?

On Thursday evening, I went through all the arguments again and allowed my Greg voice full reign to express my doubt and fears once more. But it was too late; I was resolved and the only thing now was to pluck up the courage to ask.

Steve's visit to Manchester had been successful and he was in a great mood in the office all day on Friday. He came over to my desk just before he left the office. "I'm off now, so have a good weekend. Got any plans?" he asked with a grin.

"Yeah, I've got a date tonight with a really hot man," I responded.

"Sounds fun," he replied. "Enjoy yourself and don't do anything I wouldn't." He gave me a quick peck on the cheek and headed for the door. "See you later, Rhett."

"So, did you miss me, then?" asked Steve.

We were back at Steve's flat after a fabulous Italian dinner, curled up together on the sofa. We'd scrolled through and found a 1930s' musical on the web but it was hardly riveting – and anyway there were better things to do...

"It was hell," I responded. "I was pretty miserable all week. Couldn't settle to anything. You?"

"I was lucky, I suppose. I had the distraction of the conference and the need to be polite to lots of people. But once I got back to my hotel room, it was pretty miserable – except when we Skyped, of course."

"Yes, that was good. Anyway, we're here now and I want to ask you a question." I paused, rather nervous about my next question. I was pretty sure it would be okay but you never knew… I took a deep breath and plunged ahead. "When you said last week that I could play your keyboard any time, did you really mean it?"

"Of course," he replied. "Why?"

"I've been doing a lot of thinking this week. I want to take up the music again."

"What, full time?"

"No. At least not yet. No, it's just that playing for you last week brought it all back. It reminded me how much I loved playing and singing and how I'd missed it since … since Greg. If I could maybe practise a bit, I might get back some of my confidence."

The look on Steve's face erased my anxiety. He pushed himself up so that he could turn and look at me full in the face and positively beamed. "Josh, that would be fantastic! Yes, of course you can come here and practise. We'll sort out a key for you this weekend. If nothing else came of this … us, I mean … I'd be so happy to think that it might have led you back to performing. Your voice is stunning."

I could feel myself blushing and stammered out my thanks. Steve laughed. "You're adorable when you go all shy like that." He kissed the end of my nose.

"I suppose I'm not used to all this praise and attention. I've spent the last four or five years keeping my head down and just hoping to get through the day without being noticed or upsetting anyone."

"Well you've certainly got my attention," he responded with a grin. "And you can see what it's doing to me."

I glanced down and saw his erection clearly visible in his jeans. "You should worry," I responded. "I've been trying to cope with mine since we arrived in the restaurant."

He gave me a wolfish grin. "I've got a few ideas that might help you solve the problem."

"Oh good. Do any of them involve being horizontal in your bed? Because if so, I'm certainly willing to try any or all of them."

Steve leant towards me and whispered, "You naughty boy," before initiating a kiss. After a few moments, he broke off and once again whispered in my ear. "Come on then. Bedroom. Now."

Chapter 24

Steve

We moved together towards the bedroom, hand in hand. As we crossed the threshold, I took Josh into my arms and kissed him. It was neither passionate nor urgent but gentle and caressing. As Josh moved his body so that we were touching from head to toe, I relaxed into him and fell into a dreamlike state where the only reality was holding him and kissing his soft lips.

We moved towards the bed, and started to undress each other, again gently and carefully, still with none of the urgency that had been there a week earlier. There was none of the nervousness that I'd felt then; I had no fear of things going wrong, either with Josh or in my head.

I knew that all I wanted to do was to make him feel good and secure in my arms. My joy and pleasure would come from that, not from simply satisfying an urge within me.

Once we had shed our clothes and lay down, the gentle caresses and kisses continued for a while. Then Josh moved downwards, kissing my neck and shoulders, pausing to play with my nipples for a while – a feeling that had me squirming – prompting him to look up me and grin mischievously as he stored the information about my sensitivity away for future use. Then he moved further downwards, depositing feather-light kisses over my stomach, nudging my cock with his chin as he headed further downwards until, after several base-to-tip licks, he took me into his mouth.

I let out an involuntary groan. The sensation was amazing. "God, Josh," I exclaimed, "that feels so good."

He didn't pause but looked up and gazed intently into my eyes. The eye contact made the sensations I was feeling even more intense. Then his hand cupped my balls and gently massaged them. If he wasn't careful, he'd make me come within seconds, and I didn't want to do that. I reached down and lifted him gently. "Too soon," I murmured. "Wonderful, but too soon."

He grinned. "You tasted wonderful," he said. "I shall definitely be back for some more."

I flipped him over so that I was on top and followed his example, kissing him all over and eventually moving to take him into my mouth. The sensations involved were intense – his taste, the sensual movements of his body in response and then his hand in my hair, stroking and combing through it with his fingers. I cupped his balls and moved downwards, moving between his arse cheeks to find his opening. He opened his legs to accommodate me and groaned as my finger hit the spot and stroked him gently.

After a while I broke our connection, prompting him to make a noise somewhere between a groan and a whimper. I quickly found the lube and took some on my fingers, returning to him. I massaged him again for a few seconds and then my finger entered him. He hissed with pleasure, once again writhing in a move that was rapidly becoming one of my favourites.

I pushed deeper, hooked it slightly and found the spot I was after.

"Oh God, Steve that's it! More, please."

I leant down and took him in my mouth again as I added a second finger, stretching him a little more and once again massaging his prostate. I added a third finger, which initially caused him to tense momentarily.

"Okay?" I asked, looking into his eyes. They had a dreamy quality and his whole upper body was flushed.

"Fine," he replied. "Ready for you now, Steve. Please."

I withdrew my fingers and quickly donned a condom, then applied a generous amount of lube. I positioned myself while Josh grabbed a pillow, which I placed under his hips. He spread his legs even more to give me access to him. He looked so beautiful that I had to pause to drink in the view.

His voice ended my reverie. "Steve, now. Please."

I leaned down to kiss him, entering him at the same moment. He shuddered slightly as I went past the first ring of muscle and then, as last week, stopped for a moment or two. Then I pushed a little more, and a little more until I was finally all the way in. Josh let out a deep sigh of satisfaction.

"Still all right?" I asked him.

He smiled back. "More than all right. You feel wonderful in there. I feel as if I never want to let you pull out."

I stayed still for a few more moments, revelling in the

sensations and the closeness I felt towards my boy. Then he clenched his muscle and that started me off. I began a series of gentle thrusts and we set up a relaxed, unhurried rhythm.

"Fuck, Josh, I can't last much longer."

"Me neither," he replied. "Make love to me, Steve. Come for me."

I reached for his cock and started to pump it, and our rhythm picked up speed. I felt my orgasm build and then Josh shouted as he started to come, looking at me directly, wide-eyed and so, so beautiful. As he came, he clamped down on me once again and that was enough to send me over the edge. I managed not to break our eye contact. It was the most intense sensation I'd ever felt in my life.

I leant back down for a long and passionate kiss, breaking off to look once more into his eyes. They were glistening with unshed tears. "Steve," he breathed. "That was amazing. I hope you know that I've fallen for you in a big way. I love you so much."

That was enough to set me off as well and the tears started to run down my cheeks as I smoothed his hair from his face. "Entirely mutual," I responded. "I never thought I could find this again. I'm so lucky. You're an amazing man, Josh, and you're all mine. Love doesn't even begin to describe how I feel about you."

We kissed again and then I disposed of the condom and cleaned us up before hopping back into bed and wrapping Josh into my arms again. We both fell asleep within minutes.

Chapter 25

Josh

I woke up still firmly anchored in Steve's arms. I don't think either of us had moved an inch from where we'd been when we fell asleep. I glanced across at Steve's bedside clock. It was only half past seven, far too early to get up on a Saturday morning, especially after such an intense night.

I replayed the events of the night, wriggling with pleasure a couple of times, and getting excited again. I thought about the declaration of love I had made. Despite the dangers of allowing the emotions of the moment to sweep me along, I knew that it had been more than that. I felt a deep feeling of peace and contentment when I was with Steve: everything just felt *right*.

The fact that he'd responded so quickly and with such intensity made me even more certain that I'd done the right thing.

I felt the body that was wrapped around mine begin to move and felt his lips brush my neck.

"Morning, Rhett," he said. "How ya doin'?"

"Mighty fine, Scarlett, thank you. Might fine. Y'all?"

Steve dropped the corny accent. "Never better, my Josh. Never better." He grinned up at me. "We had a good time last night, didn't we?"

"Certainly did," I agreed. "In fact, it was bloody marvellous."

"Oh, good. I wouldn't like to think that it was just me who thought that."

"No, no," I reassured him. "And what's more all the things I said – afterwards I mean – are still true in the cold light of day."

He nodded. "Me too. Not simply the passion of the moment."

He shifted his position slightly and our morning erections brushed together. And started us off again.

"Talking about passion of the moment," I said, reaching between us.

"Quite," he replied with a grin. "Gosh, that feels good. What a nice way to spend a Saturday morning."

Some time later we did actually get up, but the weather outside was foul – rain lashed the panoramic window and the wind was throwing the trees from side to side. No gentle run in the park this week. We lazed about all morning, cuddling on the sofa again after breakfast until eventually Steve made a move to stand up, reaching out a hand to help me up.

"Come on then, young Josh," he said with a grin. "If we're going to get you practising on the old Joanna, this is as good a time as any. You have a session for an hour or so whilst I sort us out some lunch."

"Sounds good to me," I replied, kissing his cheek. "I really can't wait to play your instrument again."

He grinned. "Silly sod."

We headed for Steve's study and he went through the switch-on procedure and showed me how the headphones worked and how to record my efforts if I wanted to. Eventually I sat at the instrument and once again felt the joy of my fingers moving across the keys. As had happened the previous week, I spent a little time limbering up with scales before launching into another of my favourite Gershwin numbers, "But Not For Me".

I quickly became absorbed in the melody and then in the sort of improvisation around the main tune that I loved so much. I was amazed how quickly my feel for the music was returning. So it really was like a riding a bike. I glanced up at Steve, who had remained rooted to the spot, eyes wide at the sounds coming out of his keyboard. He smiled before turning to go and start lunch. As he turned, I caught sight of a tear escaping from his eye and running down his cheek. What more appreciation from an audience could I ask for?

The Year of Awakening

Chapter 26

Steve

There was something about Josh's playing style that just got to me. I couldn't explain what it was but I had never experienced anything like it before. Admittedly I had not heard a great deal of live music and I knew that – even in these days of hi-fi and wi-fi – listening to live stuff was undoubtedly different from a recording. Maybe it was being played to personally that made a difference. I didn't know. All I understood was that hearing Josh play made me go almost literally weak at the knees.

I reluctantly turned and left the room, intent on making the promised lunch. I had to brush a tear from my eye as I left. I was clearly getting soft in my old age.

From the kitchen, I could hear his playing punctuated by breaks and resumptions in the melody and even the odd 'Oh shit' as he wrestled to rediscover his repertoire.

It was a sound, and routine, that I would get used to over the coming few weeks, as Josh spent every weekend at the flat with me, and most evenings as well. We slept together when I was at home and increasingly he stayed over to flat-sit when I was away. On several occasions it was on the tip of my tongue to ask him to move in permanently, but somehow the moment never seemed right. I couldn't work out what was missing but my gut instinct told me that something was still not there in our relationship. We needed the final piece of the jigsaw that would enable us to fit together for the rest of our lives.

I knew that he felt it too because he started to say something on a couple of occasions but then stopped and did a classic Josh deflection into humour.

Meanwhile, the hard work he put into his practice began to pay off. The breaks and resumptions grew rarer and his playing and singing became more confident. It was a joy to watch.

Around the third week in May, he broke off his session early and came to watch me making lunch. He leaned against the kitchen door jamb with a small smile on his face.

"Are you done, then?" I asked. "You were quick."

"I'm ready, Steve," he replied. "I've done as much practice and rehearsing as I can and I am back up to the standard I was a few years ago. I need an audience now to progress."

"Hey, that's great news," I enthused. "And how do you feel about the audience bit?"

He grinned. "Bloody terrified."

"Well, at least that's honest," I laughed. "Er ... can I ask a question?"

"Of course."

"How terrified? I mean in the Bristol sense of 'I'm nervous but I can do this' like you were in our meeting?

Or freak-out terrified like *Hay Fever*?"

"Mm. Good question." He paused and took a deep breath. "I think I'm Bristol terrified rather than freaked out. After all, there wouldn't be much point in all this rehearsing and practising if I didn't do anything with it, would there?"

"You could be doing it for your own satisfaction – you know, to prove to yourself that you can still do it."

"Yeah, I suppose so. But what would be the point of that?"

"You've certainly kept me entertained," I responded.

He grinned mischievously. "But apart from that, how was the music?"

"Cheeky sod."

He laughed, throwing his head back in a full-throated response, more relaxed than I'd ever seen him before. I felt my heart leap at the joy in his face.

"So what now?" I asked. "How do we get the public to respond to this amazing talent of yours?"

Josh shrugged. "More hard work, I'm afraid. Every open-mike night in every jazz and swing pub in London. Get the name out there. Get some tracks up on YouTube and Spotify – anything to get noticed, really."

"God, is it that difficult? I thought the internet had made all this stuff easy."

"As it certainly has. Compared with the old days of vinyl, it's a breeze," he said. "Trouble is, everybody else can do the same so we're still all competing to be heard."

"That sucks."

He nodded. "It certainly does, but that's the music business. If you don't want to shit, get off the pot. We all know what we're letting ourselves in for. That's the point, though, isn't it? Letting ourselves go and being honest – against a pattern of deceit."

I could not help but shudder at his words. Why was my Josh putting himself out there, risking rejection, heckling and the money grubbers? Surely he'd be safer staying with Pearson Frazer and being a successful consultant?

With a shock that was almost a physical jolt, I realised that I was thinking along precisely the same lines as Josh's ex had. Maybe it was because he felt so strongly about Josh that Greg became over-protective and in the process almost destroyed the man he loved. Given how easy it was for me to fall into the same thought process, I had no doubt that this sort of behaviour might be all too common.

Well, that was not going to happen to Josh and me. I knew that performing was in Josh's blood – he really was born to it. It was only when he was at a keyboard, or working on stage in some capacity, that he truly came alive. That was what mattered. In that moment I knew that, if necessary, I would stand aside in order to let him achieve his goal.

I finished making lunch and we sat down to eat. Our conversation resumed its normal light, jokey tone.

"Oh, by the way, I had an e-mail from my mum this morning," Josh remarked.

"How are things at home?"

"Fine, but Mum and Dad are a bit miffed that they haven't seen me since Christmas. They want me to go for Spring Bank Holiday weekend. Would you mind?"

"Of course not," I replied immediately, determined to keep my resolutions about giving him space. "You certainly ought to go – seeing them is important because they won't be here forever. I often wish I'd made more effort to see my mum and dad before I lost them."

He nodded. "It's also important because I want to tell them about you."

I cocked an eyebrow. "Really?"

"Yeah, absolutely. Mum knows there's something going on in my life, but she doesn't know what yet. And she doesn't know about the singing yet."

"They know you're gay, right?"

"Of course. I've been out with them since I was sixteen. But they got very concerned after Greg ... you know, me dropping out of drama school and everything and them having to come and rescue me. They're still very protective and worry about what I'm up to."

"Understandably," I said. "That must all have been really upsetting for them."

"Yeah, it was. So, as I say, I haven't said anything about a new boyfriend, about you. And I don't want to tell them over the phone. I need to do it in person, to explain."

His words petered out in confusion and he blushed.

"About teaming up with an old crock like me, you mean?" I asked with a laugh.

His expression hardened. "You are *not* an old crock, Steve! Oh, God, please don't say that, even in jest. You are a very attractive and fit man at the height of his powers..." He grinned and waggled his eyebrows at me. "As you proved again last night."

"I get all that, but there is an age gap and we've got to recognise that it might seem a little odd to some people – particularly your parents. Tell me, how old is your dad?"

"Forty-seven," Josh replied, blushing again. "He and Mum married young, you see."

"Crikey. That means he's only five years older than me."

He nodded.

"That's not going to go down very well, is it, Josh?"

He shook his head. "It's difficult. Which is why I have to go and tell them in person and explain. Convince them that this time it's right."

"Yeah, I understand that entirely. I'd offer to come with you but that might only make matters worse."

He smiled. "I'd love you to meet them and I do think that they'll love you. They'll certainly love what you've done for my confidence in helping me play and sing again. But let's take it one step at a time, okay?"

As was our usual pattern, Josh headed home around teatime on the Sunday, allowing us to prepare for the week ahead and him to spend some time with Robbie and Malcolm on their only day of rest during the week.

The flat felt so empty when he'd gone. I knew that I ought to do a bit of preparation for the following day but I couldn't settle, so I headed for my wing chair. The sun was just starting to set so the view was cast in what I could only think of as a rosy glow. The sky was speckled with lines of small clouds, dark grey against the pink-orange sky. It was spectacular.

I had been unsettled by our conversation at lunchtime about Josh's parents. What would they think of our relationship? What would they think of me? The fact that

I was only five years younger than Josh's father reminded me of my own concerns about our age difference when I'd first realised how strong my feelings were for Josh.

I tried to imagine how I would feel in that situation. I would not be keen for a son of mine to get together with somebody so much older. I wondered what effect parental disapproval would have on Josh and his feelings for me. It was not that I doubted his love but any difficulty between him and his parents would be upsetting and unnecessarily complicated. As I had learned over the last few months, Josh's self-confidence was still fragile after what that bastard Greg had done to him. If he was to succeed as a performer, he would need every ounce of self-belief that he could muster.

In the end I forced myself to relax; there was no point in worrying. Nothing I could do between now and next weekend could affect the reactions of two people who I'd never met. I knew that, like me, his parents cared deeply about Josh and wanted the best for him. We might disagree on what that would be, but in the end I would just have to go with the flow and help Josh to deal with the consequences.

The Year of Awakening

Chapter 27

Josh

As I drove down to my parents' house in Kent, I could not recall a time when I had been so nervous about seeing them. The Friday evening traffic through South London was tedious but, once I was clear of the suburbs, I revelled in the relative quiet of the country lanes that my route took me along, across the eastern end of the North Downs, down the southern escarpment and onto the Weald.

It was a lovely spring evening. The hedges were full of bluebells and other spring flowers and, whenever I stopped at a junction, the air was full of birdsong. It reminded me of why I had become passionate about preserving the environment and had joined Pearson Frazer in the first place.

The drive helped me to relax and the familiar sight of the roads leading towards the village where I grew up brought a smile to my face. I thought how much Steve would love the area when eventually I brought him down here.

As the church clock struck eight, I swung the car round the corner past the cricket pitch on the village green and into my parent's drive. The crunch of the gravel must have alerted Mum because, by the time I had parked and grabbed my bag, the front door was open and she was standing there to greet me.

It was good to be home.

"So, tell me about how things are really going." This was my mother. We sat over the remains of dinner, finishing our wine as we'd done countless times before over the years. It was a time for relaxed conversation, often peppered with jokes or funny stories about our day.

Except tonight I could not relax. The conversation over dinner had been tentative and stilted, definitely not the Ashcroft family style.

Well, here goes. In for a penny...

I took a deep breath and began. "Actually it's been quite an intense and busy few months – hence my not being able to get down to see you both. Two things have happened. Firstly, I've got a new boyfriend, and secondly, I've started playing again."

My mother's face lit up. "Oh that's fantastic news! Josh, I'm so pleased."

I suspected that she was much more interested in my starting to perform than my love life and this was confirmed by her next question. "So how did you come to start again? What are you doing about it?"

My father caught my eye and rolled his. "Jean, Josh has just said he's got a new boyfriend. I think he might be more interested in that fact than in playing the piano."

"Oh, yes. Sorry," Mum said with a smile. "Tell us all about him."

"You remember at Christmas I told you about my new boss, Steve Frazer."

"Yes. You had a bit of trouble relating to him at first, didn't you?" Dad asked.

"Absolutely," I replied. "It was very difficult – but then we hit it off and things have developed from there."

"Wait a minute, Josh," Dad replied. "Are you telling me that you're dating your *boss*?"

I nodded.

It was my mother's turn to intervene. "But isn't he quite a bit older than you, dear?"

"Yes, he's fourteen years older, Mum, but it doesn't matter. I absolutely love him, and we get on like a house on fire."

The atmosphere in the room chilled noticeably. Rather abruptly, Mum got up and left the room, saying quietly, "I'll go and make the coffee."

Dad, who had been staring at his placemat, looked up suddenly and caught my eye. "So, he's what? Forty-two?"

I nodded. "Yup."

"Christ, Josh. He's only five years younger than me."

I nodded and smiled, trying to be reassuring. "Steve pointed that out last weekend. He was worried that it would freak you out."

"Good of him."

Oh, dear. This is not going very well.

"Why him?" asked Mum, returning to the room with the coffee tray. She was a little red-eyed but otherwise seemed okay.

I shrugged. "Why anybody? Because he's very good looking and I find him attractive. He's fit and active. We get on well together and seem to have the same sense of humour. Because he's been on his own for over twenty years and he chose me to be the first person to share his life since he lost his previous partner in tragic circumstances. And most of all because it just feels right. I can't really explain what I mean by that but I just know that he's my rock and that I want to spend the rest of my life with him."

There was a pause while they took all that in. Before they spoke again, I had a further thought. "You two know more than anyone how difficult life was for me after the business with Greg, how I didn't want to go out and certainly not to date anybody. Steve was the first person to change that – to make me want to think about anything other than just getting through the day without being noticed. You should know, Mum, that Steve was the one who inspired me to start playing again and gave me the confidence to succeed."

My father smiled. "That's quite a testimonial, Josh."

My mother nodded her agreement, her eyes filling once more. "It is."

I relaxed, feeling the first signs of the atmosphere warming once more. I had one more thing to say, which might give them too much information, but the psychological angle to all this suddenly struck me.

"And in case it has crossed either of your minds, my attraction to Steve is because of who and what he is, not some Freudian stuff about father or mother substitutes. I love Steve because of who he is as a person, not because he represents something else. To me, he's an attractive, sexy, very clever but rather vulnerable man who just happens to be a few years older than me."

"All we ever want for you is to be happy, Josh," replied my mother. "If Steve makes you happy then I am too."

"That goes for me as well," Dad interjected. He paused and then smiled. "So when can we meet him?"

I closed my eyes and took a deep breath – not quite a sigh of relief, but almost. I was fairly certain that everything would be okay now. I was confident that once they met Steve they would understand how I felt and seeing us together would show them how strong the bonds between us were.

Once the evening was over and I was in my room, I sent Steve a quick text.

JOSH: >>*Mission accomplished. They want to meet you soon.*
STEVE:>> *Well done! Hope not too difficult.*
JOSH: >> *One dodgy moment but my superb advocacy won the day.*
STEVE:> *Hmm. Modest too I see, Rhett.*
JOSH:> *Always, Scarlett. Modest and retiring, just like you.*

We sent a few more silly messages back and forth but eventually said good night. I got ready for bed and slipped between the sheets, on my own for the first time for a few weeks. But I was not awake long enough for it to matter; the stress and tension involved in this evening's discussion had left me exhausted and I slept long and deeply.

The rest of the weekend was spent in harmony. Mum, Dad and I slipped back into our old intimacy. It was very relaxing. I told them about my first open-mike night the following week and they promised to try to be there.

I played and sang for them on Sunday evening, which

they loved. Mum confirmed what I knew in my heart of hearts: namely that I had got back my mojo and that my performance standards were as high as they had ever been.

"If Steve has done that for you, darling, I will love him forever."

Now I couldn't say fairer than that.

Chapter 28

Steve

There were fifteen of us: virtually all the staff from the office, plus Josh's housemates and a couple of his cousins, assembled in a South London pub waiting for the open-mike night to start. This was Josh's debut as an aspiring jazz musician and his first appearance on any stage since that disastrous night at drama school seven years earlier.

The venue was fascinating, a real old-fashioned Victorian pub with big rooms, lots of etched glass on the windows and a beautiful period interior. The original brass chandeliers and wall lights sparkled, their tungsten bulbs casting a comfortable light. Just walking in got several 'wows' from our party and the bar staff gave us a great welcome.

It was nearly showtime and Josh was sitting with us, awaiting his turn. He had been given a slot third in from the start and would be allowed fifteen minutes, enough to do three numbers from his repertoire. It wasn't much but it was a start, and certainly easier than going from completely cold to performing a full ninety-minute set in a club.

We'd got him a portable keyboard and small folding stool especially for this type of venue. It might not be as good as a full piano but we knew that there would be some venues that would not have one and others where the instrument would be virtually unplayable, so a portable instrument had seemed a sensible compromise.

We had worked out which three songs Josh would sing. He'd wanted an upbeat number to start with, followed by a ballad and finishing with another upbeat song to end on a high note. We'd batted ideas back and forth all over the weekend and eventually he'd decided to open with a version of 'Fly Me to the Moon' with the same swinging beat as the famous Nelson Riddle arrangement for Sinatra. The slow number would be 'Someone to Watch Over Me.' Finally, in tribute to his love for the show *Guys and Dolls*, he'd wow them with 'Luck Be a Lady Tonight.'

Certainly with a group of fifteen supporters in the audience, he was guaranteed a good reception from our part of the room. With luck, others would follow our lead. I so wanted this to be a success for him so that he could show the rest of the world the talent that I heard in the flat every night. Josh's parents had not been able to make it after all but had sent their good wishes. I must confess that I was rather relieved – this was not the best of circumstances for a first meeting.

As the second act's time slot came to an end, I could see Josh going paler and paler just as he had before our meeting that day in Bristol. I reached out and rubbed his back above his waistline.

"You're going to be great, Rhett," I whispered. "This is a superb venue and they're going to love you."

He nodded and gave me a rather wan smile. "Thanks, Scarlett. Just what I needed."

The pub was now around three-quarters full and, to judge by the boisterous reception the first two acts received, Josh would be fine. Robbie and I helped him to set up and after a couple of minutes he was ready. He shut his eyes and took a deep breath, then looked up at the master of ceremonies and smiled, giving him a nod.

"Ladieees and gentlemeeen. Our next act is making his debut here at the Flying Pig, so let's give a real big snorting welcome to ... Josh Ash ... CROFT.;."

Josh took his cue and launched straight into the opening bars of the song. It was a perfect choice, because most of the audience knew it and quickly recognised the arrangement. It was also good because the voice came in quickly. Once he started to sing, I could tell that all was going to be well; the room hushed as this warm, golden voice swung into action. By the time he'd got to the end of the first verse, the audience was hooked.

There were hollers and cheers as he ended his opening number and not just from the Pearson Frazer tables. Josh grinned at us as he introduced his second song. The Gershwin number was an absolute standard, having been recorded by virtually all the big stars from the late twenties onwards. He did the full version, including the rarely performed introduction. Once again I could feel the audience being drawn in and, by the time he got to the first verse proper, you could have heard a pin drop.

At the line about *hurrying along please,* he sought and found my eyes, singing directly to me. I felt my eyes sting as he winked and then focused back on the keyboard for the last chorus. Once again the room erupted at the end of the song but he only gave the briefest of acknowledgements before launching straight into the introduction of 'Luck Be a Lady.' By the time he got to the first chorus, virtually the whole room was swaying in time to the up-tempo song. It really was a special moment and I was sure that everybody in the room that night would remember it in years to come.

The audience rose to its feet at the end and clapped and cheered for what seemed an age before the MC restored some semblance of order. Despite the clamours for more, Josh had used up his allotted slot and had to give way to the next act.

We packed up his keyboard and returned to our table. Josh was alight, bouncing on his toes, eyes shining and a grin as wide as could be. He stood close to me and grabbed my hand. "Was I all right?" he breathed into my ear.

"Beyond praise," I responded. "Bloody brilliant! Josh, I am so proud of you. Are you okay?"

"Never better. I'm so relieved to have got that one over. It'll be all right from now on, I just know it."

The rest of the evening flew by. Josh was mobbed by excited audience members wanting to talk or take a selfie, and our group sat basking in reflected glory. As closing time arrived and we tried unsuccessfully to get Josh away, Barbara got close.

"The boy did good," she said.

"Yeah, he's a natural, isn't he?"

"You know you'll lose him..." Panic gripped my heart for a moment and a shiver sped through my body. She must have seen something in my face. "From the firm, silly," she added. "He's born to perform, not to be an environmental consultant."

I nodded. "You're right, of course. It's inevitable. A shame because he's a bloody good consultant too, but there we are."

She may not have meant to but she'd set the wheels in motion. If he left the firm, why should he stay in touch with me? We'd be moving in completely different circles. If Josh was successful, which I was sure he would be, he'd be working at night, often away on tour, close to fellow musicians and others in the business.

Of course we'd drift apart. It was inevitable. Panic gripped my stomach – how could I possibly survive that? Losing not one but two people who had become so important to me. I needed to be decisive about it and act before my heart got broken for the second time.

The Year of Awakening

Chapter 29

Josh

I knew something was wrong as soon as Steve and I got back to his place. He'd been effusive in his praise of the performance and ecstatic about the reception I received. But it was all curiously flat – almost as if he were on autopilot – and his eyes, normally so expressive, were dull and remote. He was physically remote too; there was no brushing hands or kissing of temples tonight. When I moved in for a hug, I only received the briefest of clasps.

I was coming down from the buzz I had got from performing, especially to such a responsive and enthusiastic audience. My adrenalin rush was subsiding and I was starting to feel tired, but my instincts told me that I needed to confront whatever was going on in Steve's mind.

"I can see the wheels going round, Steve. What's going on in that head of yours?"

"Nothing, nothing at all," he replied brusquely. "Just a bit tired, that's all. Been a long day for both of us."

I put my head on one side and looked at him. "Steve Frazer, I haven't known you for that long, but I do know a big fib when I see one. Come on, out with it. Who or what upset you tonight?"

"I tell you, nobody did," he replied, his voice taking on a slightly irritated tone. "It's nothing. Now, can we leave it, please? I need some sleep."

I shook my head and spat out the words. "No, we fucking can't, Steve. We need to talk these things out, not let them fester and poison the atmosphere. Something. Happened. Out there. Now tell me what the fuck it was."

He fixed me with an angry stare, his piercing blue eyes acting like electric drills into my brain. But I stood my ground. Bless him, he blinked first and I was horrified to see his eyes fill with tears. What the fuck?

"It was Barbara. At the end of your act. She said I'd lose you now."

"She said *what*?"

"She meant from the firm, Josh. You'd be such a success, she said, that you wouldn't want to be a boring old consultant anymore and you'd leave the firm."

I relaxed slightly. I could understand what she meant, but it was hardly the moment...

"Anyway," Steve resumed, "it set me thinking. If that happened and you became a full-time musician, I'd probably lose you altogether because we'd lead separate lives and grow farther apart. And then I thought about that, and losing you like I lost Jamie and..." He stopped in mid-sentence and looked at me, his eyes still full.

I reached out and took him into a hug. "Oh, Steve, you daft bugger!" I said. "I would *never* do that to you."

He relaxed slightly in my arms but then spoke again. "But how can you say that with such certainty?"

"Because I *know*, Steve. You have to understand that you are my rock: the fact that I'm performing at all is down to you. I couldn't do any of it without you at my back. So if at any stage we have to make a choice between us as a unit and my career, then my choice will always be for you and what we've built together over the last few months."

He held me at arms' length for a moment and looked me directly in the eye. His own once again sparkled with unshed tears. "Gosh," he said, "and you really mean that, don't you?"

I nodded. "Oh I do, Steve, I do. You may as well make up your mind that you're stuck with me now for the duration."

He blinked and drew me even more tightly into his embrace. He tilted his head and his mouth met mine in a hard, passionate kiss. He pulled away and buried his face in my neck. "Oh God, I love you so much, Josh."

"And I you," I replied. "Now come to bed and I'll prove just how much."

We turned toward the bedroom, arms still round each other, but our progress was brought to a stop as the phone started to ring.

"Who the hell...?" said Steve as he moved to the desk to pick up the handset. It was the first time I'd known the landline phone to ring in his flat in all the times I'd been here. People always used his mobile.

Steve picked up. "Steve Frazer... Oh, hi, Rob. Good to hear from you...' Steve looked up at me and frowned. "Rob, I am sorry. What happened? ... A stroke, you say...?"

I worked out that the call was about Steve's aunt in Yorkshire and, from the way the conversation was going, it was pretty clear that she had died. I moved to the desk, took Steve's hand and squeezed it. He quickly squeezed back but then turned his back on me and carried on talking with his cousin.

I headed for the bedroom and started to get ready for sleep, feeling fairly low both in sympathy for Steve but also fearing the consequences of the news on his fairly fragile mental state. As I got into bed, I could still hear the rumble of Steve's voice talking to Rob on the phone.

Eventually, exhausted after the excitements of the evening – God, how long ago that now seemed – I dozed off to sleep.

Some time later, I awoke suddenly. The lamp was still on as I had left it and the other side of the bed was still empty. Steve's bedside alarm read four thirty. My heart sank.

Chapter 30

Steve

Rob called to tell me that Auntie Meg had died that evening, after having a stroke at home at teatime. Though she was rushed to hospital, they could not save her and she had another seizure around nine, which finished her off. He was ringing from the hospital on his mobile, which had a poor signal, so it was difficult to hear and I had to concentrate very hard on his voice.

It was clear from the way Josh came over and took my hand that he had picked up on what was going on. I was grateful for the feel of his hand but I had to let it go to concentrate on what Rob was saying.

It seemed that Auntie Meg had not been feeling well for a few days but would not do anything about it. Despite being eighty, she still lived on her own and was fiercely independent. Owning up to illness would have seemed like weakness to her, plus there was the additional risk of her being told that she could no longer manage on her own.

Yes, Rob was all right. Owen was with him at the hospital – he'd just been coming off shift when they got the call.

A longer conversation was well nigh impossible given the poor line so we agreed to talk the following day. Of course I would go to the funeral, I reassured him, though my stomach started to tie itself into knots at the prospect of returning to Long Garfield for the first time in more than twenty years. We ended the call and I looked round to see that Josh had headed off to bed. That was fine; he must have been exhausted after the show.

I, on the other hand, felt wide awake. My mind was racing and I needed to come to terms with the news and all that heading north again implied. Seeing all those people in the village I had fled from all those years ago was a daunting prospect.

"I need a drink," I told myself and went to the sideboard. I poured myself a large measure of single malt and flopped down on the sofa, staring blankly into space, remembering.

Auntie Meg was the last of her generation and the only person who had known me before the court case and my time in prison. She had known – and loved – Jamie as well and for that reason alone she was precious to me. In addition, she cherished me in the months and years after I came out of prison. She didn't offer to take me in because she knew I couldn't face going back to Long Garfield again, but she phoned constantly, made occasional visits to London and sent letters – long, chatty, helpful, funny and insightful. Above all else, she had sustained me during those difficult early years in London. And now she was gone.

I hadn't even had the chance to tell her about Josh and my renewed hopes for the future. Thinking of Josh, I knew that I ought to go and check on him, to make sure he was okay. I got up from the sofa and walked through to our bedroom. Sure enough, he was stretched out, fast asleep and snoring softly. He looked so adorable it made my eyes sting. I leaned over and kissed his temple then went back to the living room, taking my usual place in the chair by the window, whisky bottle at my side.

I knew then that I could not possibly follow through on any resolution to walk away from him. I needed to get Auntie Meg's funeral done with and lay any other ghosts that crept out of the woodwork in Long Garfield. Maybe then we could get on with the rest of our lives. But I had to do this next bit on my own; I couldn't expect Josh to get involved and, to be honest, introducing my new boyfriend in these circumstances just felt wrong.

The second glass of whisky began to have its effect and at long last my mind slowed down. Not for the first time in my life, I settled down in my chair and put my head back. Within moments, I was fast asleep.

The Year of Awakening

Chapter 31

Josh

When I came out of the bedroom to check on Steve, I found him fast asleep in his big wing chair, empty glass by his side. I went round and switched off all the lights except one in case he woke and wanted to find his way to bed. At least he seemed peaceful even though the loss of his aunt must be hurting him.

I was worried about how he would react to her death and, presumably, the need to go back to his childhood home for the funeral. I was sure he would want to do that on his own and to an extent I could understand that. At the same time, I knew that his wounds had not yet healed. If nothing else, his reaction to poor Barbara's innocent remark tonight demonstrated that he was still fearful that people – and especially I – would walk away and leave him.

Perhaps I could persuade him to let me go with him, or at least be somewhere nearby in case he needed me. Meanwhile I was faced with the more immediate question of whether to wake Steve and persuade him to come to bed or leave him in the chair. I decided on the latter and fetched a blanket with which to cover him.

As I tucked it round him, I couldn't resist the temptation to reach across and kiss him on the temple. He stirred for moment, and said, "Love you, Josh."

I went back to bed a happy bunny.

Steve shook me awake the following morning. He was fully dressed and ready for the office. "I let you sleep as long as possible," he said with a smile. "But it's eight-thirty and you really ought to turn up for work at some point this morning."

"Thanks, I needed the sleep. Hey, are you okay? I am sorry about your aunt – I would have said it last night but I was so tired...'

"Thanks, Josh. No, I'm all right, I think. It made me think, though. I suppose I'll have to go back now. And thanks for the blanket, by the way." He smiled. "And the little kiss. Felt just right."

"My pleasure," I responded. "I decided to leave you in the chair rather than wake you up to bring you to bed. I hope that was okay."

Steve smiled ruefully. "It's not the first time I've slept all night in that chair and I dare say it won't be the last. No, it was fine, Josh. Now, I'd better go and earn us some money if I'm going to keep you in the style to which you want to become accustomed."

"Okay. I'll get ready and be round shortly. But Steve?"
"Yeah?"
"Let me come with you. To the funeral, I mean. I don't

want you facing it all alone."

He frowned. "No, it'll be okay. Thanks, but I need to handle this bit myself."

He turned and left. He had reacted as I'd expected but I was not convinced. I needed to talk to Barbara about this.

The Year of Awakening

Chapter 32

Steve

The next few days were frantic at work, with a couple of deadlines looming at the end of the week. In many ways that was a good thing because it helped me to shove Auntie Meg and the funeral to the back of my mind.

Rob rang me again the following evening, from home this time so at least we could hear each other. The funeral was fixed for the following Tuesday afternoon. That was okay with me but it meant that I would have to travel up by train from central London after a meeting at lunchtime on Monday. I would have to leave immediately after the wake in order to be back for a meeting first thing on the Wednesday morning.

There seemed even less point in taking Josh with me, even though I was still tempted by his offer to accompany me. The idea of having at least one friendly face, someone who had my back, was appealing. I dismissed the thought. Rob would be there with his husband Owen, so I'd be okay, I was sure.

Thus it was that I left London at teatime on the Monday, riding initially to Leeds where I would change onto the Settle and Carlisle line for the trip to my old home. I had arranged for Rob to meet me at the nearest railhead in Settle. He insisted that I should stay with him and Owen for the night rather than the hotel I had planned for.

From the moment the train left King's Cross I was very nervous and began to regret not bringing Josh with me. I had brought some work to do on the train and it successfully distracted me most of the way to Leeds. Working was much more difficult on the local train northwards, though, so I was once again free to speculate, worry and generally allow my stomach to tie itself into ever tighter knots.

The sun was low in the sky by the time we arrived at Settle and the moon was visible as well. The railway was tucked into one side of the valley and it provided a striking view across to the northern outskirts of the town and the village of Giggleswick across the river. It was a breath-taking sight.

My cousin was on the platform to greet me and immediately wrapped me in a big hug. Though we had not seen each other very often, we had become close during our frequent telephone conversations about his grandmother's welfare. I had not met Rob's husband Owen yet; he wasn't with Rob at the station.

"Owen was sorry not to be here to meet you," Rob explained. "He was down to work today and couldn't manage to do a swap, especially as he's managed to get tomorrow off for the funeral."

"Yeah," I sympathised. "It's tough, especially at short notice. It was a bit difficult for me – hence this brief visit."

"You must come and stay for longer in the autumn," Rob responded. "Bring Josh and stay with us for a week or two. We can help you get re-acquainted with your home county," he added.

"That would be great," I replied, hoping that I sounded more enthusiastic than I felt. The longer I stood there, the more panicky I felt. I started to tremble and feel short of breath.

Rob noticed and looked at me with concern. "Come on, Steve, let's get you away from here and up to our house. You'll be okay there, I'm sure."

I nodded my thanks and gave him a half smile.

He saw me across the footbridge and out to his car and we set off across the valley. Rob and Owen lived in a converted farmhouse and barn high in the hills west of Settle. The air was much fresher up here and it was sufficiently far away from any memories for my anxieties to ease again.

Owen was just pulling into the drive as we got home and he got out of his car to greet me warmly. "Welcome back to Yorkshire," he said in a big, booming, bass voice. Then he dropped his tone and spoke for my ears only. "And thanks for coming to this. I know it means a lot to Rob. I know it'll be difficult for you tomorrow but I want to know that we'll look after you and keep you safe."

I was puzzled momentarily by his choice of words but decided not to question him. He led me into a house that was breathtakingly beautiful. It had started life as a traditional Dales farmhouse, with the home for the farmer and his family at one end and a barn for the animals at the other. The barn had been converted into a spacious studio for Rob's videography and music-recording business, with editing suites and a control room off to the side. It was a spectacular double-height space and I gazed at it in wonder and admiration.

"Nice, isn't it?" said Owen with a grin. "Finally finished all the work two weeks ago – it's taken us three years but boy, has it been worth it!"

I nodded, "I remember Rob telling me about it the last time I saw him in London. I think you'd just bought the place then. It really is fabulous. I wish Josh was here – he would love this."

"Supper's nearly ready," called Rob from the kitchen. "Come through and Owen'll sort out some drinks."

Rob was a good cook so supper was delicious, and we chatted away happily ... up to a point. Somehow there was a bit of an odd atmosphere; it was as if they were holding back on something. Their conversation was rather stilted. Each of them seemed to think carefully about what he was going to say in case he put his foot in it.

I pretended not to notice and the evening went reasonably smoothly. It was heart-warming to see how close Rob and Owen were and how happy they seemed together. I was sure my aunt would have approved; in fact, I knew from conversations with her that she most heartily did.

Owen was – to use the vernacular phrase – built like a brick shithouse. He stood over six feet four and packed a huge amount of muscle. Despite this, he was clearly the most gentle of people and had the kindest face you could ever wish to see.

We retreated to their snug after supper. It had grown

cool after sunset, so Rob put a match to the wood-burner and we sat in front of it, toasting our toes.

It was Rob who introduced the subject they had obviously been on tenterhooks about. "Steve, I'm sorry if we seemed a bit anxious tonight but the fact is that we've got a letter for you from my grandma. I know it'll be difficult for you but if she says the same as in the letter she left for us, you need to know about it."

I had a one-word question. "Jamie?"

Rob nodded and handed me the envelope. The handwriting was recognisably Meg's, though it had got rather spidery in her old age. I used the letter opener he handed me to slit open the envelope and took the sheets out, uttering a silent prayer.

Rob and Owen quietly left the room. "Shout when you need us," Rob said.

The Year of Awakening

Chapter 33

Josh

Having said goodbye to Steve as he left the flat for the office that morning, I did not see him again before he set off for Yorkshire. Though I sat at my desk with my computer turned on, I achieved virtually nothing all day and eventually gave up around three, deciding to take some flexi-hours off.

Before leaving the building, I stuck my head round Barbara's office door to tell her that I was going.

"Whatever's the matter, Josh? You look as if you've lost a shilling and found sixpence," she said with a smile.

"Nothing really, it's just that I've got this uneasy feeling about Steve in the pit of my stomach. I know I'm being silly but I can't help it. I wish he'd let me go with him – at least I could have stayed nearby."

"Why are you so worried?"

"For a start, he's going back to his home village for the first time in over twenty years and I know he's nervous about that. And then there's all the other business."

"You mean Jamie and the court case?"

I nodded. "You know about that, then?"

"He told me years ago, when we first met – and then only the bare outlines. But I know that he's never got over it." She paused. "At least until you came along and swept him off his feet."

I laughed this off but could not prevent the blush that suffused my cheeks. "From what he's told me it was all pretty traumatic. I'm worried that he won't cope well, especially if somebody says something nasty. You know what he's like if he has one of his meltdown moments."

Barbara rolled her eyes. "Do I ever?" She laughed briefly and then grew serious. "Look, why don't you at least head north? Go and get the next train to Leeds and you should be able to get as far as Skipton. I'll get you a hotel for the night. At least that way you'll only be half an hour away."

"Do you actually know where he is? He's never told me the name of the village or anything. I don't even know what his name was before he changed it."

She nodded. "The village is called Long Garfield. The nearest station is Settle, I think." She went over to her filing cabinet. "Steve's original name was ... let me see... ah, there it is. We had to tell the bank what his original name was. Yes, here it is: he was called Paul Steven Bates." She put the file away and turned to me again. "Now off you go. The trains to Leeds are every half hour. I'll text you the hotel details as soon as I get them."

I dashed home to pack a few things then grabbed my bag and headed for King's Cross. I treated myself to a first-class ticket, which meant I would get a meal on the train, and we left London just after six. As luck would have it, the train went through to Skipton and Barbara had found me a room in a smallish hotel just opposite the station.

I relaxed. At least I wouldn't be far away if some sort of crisis did break.

The Year of Awakening

Chapter 34

Steve

I drew the sheets of notepaper from the envelope. Judging by the number of pages, it was a longish letter. I again thought about Josh and realised how much I wished he was here, holding my hand or cuddling up to me. I couldn't resist shooting him a quick text.

STEVE:>>Where are you?

There was a short pause then my phone pinged.

JOSH:>> Skipton.

STEVE:>> WTF? Why?

JOSH:>> Just to be on hand. Love you too much to abandon you to the heathens.

STEVE:>>Come and stay? If it's all right with Rob?

Josh replied with a heart-shaped emoticon. I called to Rob.

"Finished already?" he asked.

"No. Haven't started, actually. I just texted Josh to see if he was okay and it seems he's in Skipton – I'm not fit to be let out on my own, apparently. I wondered if he could join us?"

"Of course. I'll get Owen to go and fetch him. Where is he?"

I shook my head. "There's no need – I am sure he can get a cab. He'll just need the address."

"Text me his number and I'll sort him out," said my cousin with a smile. "I look forward to meeting him."

He went off and I sat down again in the snug. I closed my eyes and let out a sigh of relief, then the full import of what had just happened hit me. Tonight had clinched it; any thought that I could survive without Josh in my life was just ridiculous. I smiled to myself. Why should that come as a surprise?

"Enough, Frazer," I told myself. "Read the bloody letter."

My darling Paul

Sorry, I know that's not your name any more but I still think of you as my little Paul, my favourite nephew. I wish you still were, because that would mean that none of the story I'm going to tell you would ever have happened.

I thought I ought to write this all down for you, as I'm not sure how much time I've got left, and it's important that you of all people should know my story. I've written one to my own darling grandson, too, so you can compare notes and work out what you might do. I'm sure Rob's lovely boy Owen will help out too, bless him.

For a long time after Jamie died, both while you were in prison and then after you went to London, I puzzled and puzzled about things, especially the suicide verdict. I knew it wasn't right – Jamie just wasn't the type to do that. Anyway, I'd had a really long talk with him the day before it all happened. He loved you so much, Paul, and couldn't wait for you to serve your time and come back to him. There was just no way he could have contemplated killing himself.

I broke off at this point and put the letter down. I couldn't read any more for the moment because my eyes were too full. I felt completely torn: on the one hand, my aunt's words acted as a comfort blanket, reinforcing my own hope and belief that Jamie had not left me deliberately and that he would have kept his promise to wait for me if he possibly could have done. On the other hand, the whole act of reading the letter felt as if somebody was jabbing me with a stiletto, reopening old wounds. The pain was excruciating.

I wiped my eyes, breathed deeply and prepared to continue reading. Rob stuck his head round the door to say that Josh was getting a cab and should be here in about half an hour.

"Are you okay?" he asked.

I shook my head. "Not really."

"I know," he said, smiling gently and giving my shoulder a squeeze. He left me to it and I resumed reading Meg's letter.

I didn't know what to do. As you know, Jamie's mum and dad were in shock and your parents were still coping with you being in prison, so I couldn't really talk to any of them.

So in the end I went to see Derek Heath. You may remember him, he's a solicitor in Settle. We've known the family for years. I said my two pennyworth to him. He saw my argument and said he'd do what he could, but came back to me a few weeks later and said he couldn't get anywhere. The inquest had been held and a cause of death established so the police had closed their file and wouldn't say any more. The coroner would be most reluctant to reopen the case without compelling new evidence, which we didn't have. He thought the police reaction was a bit odd, but he didn't have any legal status since he was not acting directly for the next of kin.

I went to see Jamie's mum and dad then but they wouldn't listen. His mum said she didn't want to create any trouble. Nothing could bring Jamie back so what did it matter?

I broke off again, remembering Jamie's mum. A loving and gentle woman, she had been very kind to me and treated me as part of their family for my entire time with Jamie. She had supported him so well throughout my prosecution and I knew how secure he'd felt in his home life. I could only speculate what it would be like to lose your only son in such circumstances.

I dashed more tears from my eyes and carried on.

Jamie's dad said he would help if he could but he couldn't go against Mary's wishes. That was the night he told me that they were thinking of emigrating to make a new start. I couldn't blame them.

Then something odd happened. I got a visit from Inspector Hardwick at Settle. He said he'd heard that I'd been 'making waves' over Jamie's death and that since it was none of my business I should shut up and forget about it, for the sake of Jamie's parents and to help the village 'calm down' after the recent

*'scandal.' God, Paul, I was so furious it's a wonder
I didn't thump him. I'd known John Hardwick since
childhood and he always was a pompous bastard.*

I broke off again, smiling at Meg's turn of phrase. She
was always forthright in her views about people, especially
her fellow residents in the village. One thing about Meg
was that you always knew where you stood. I remembered
John Hardwick as a remote figure, sinister in his uniform
with lots of pips on the shoulders. Hadn't he had had a son
the same age as Jamie? Yes, he had: Ned, that was it. Ned
Hardwick. Big, beefy and bull-headed, just like his father.

I read on, fascinated now and with the glimmer of an
idea about where this narrative might be going.

*So I was stuck; there was nothing I could do, so I let
the matter drop. And there things lay until three years
ago. I was reading about a case in the local paper
where a forensic expert, Roberts by name, had col-
luded with a policeman to get somebody convicted.
Roberts was sent to prison for perjury and perverting
the course of justice. I recognised the name.*

*I rang Derek Heath and got him to check – yes, it
was the same Roberts who'd given evidence at Jamie's inquest. He'd also found out that they thought
they knew who the policeman was who worked with
Roberts on all the cases round here. Nobody was saying who it was yet, but a team had been appointed to
review all Roberts' cases. Derek couldn't even get a
hint about the identity of the policeman under investigation.*

*Three weeks later, he rang me to say that the team
investigating the Roberts case had agreed to pick up
Jamie's inquest as part of their investigation. They*

hadn't considered it before, because there had been no criminal case involved, just a verdict of suicide. That's where we stand, though Derek rang me the other week to let me know that the new file about the policeman – including Jamie's case – was now with the Crown Prosecution Service.

I've written all this down for Rob and for you so that you know and can take up the cudgels. I haven't been feeling too good lately and something tells me my time may soon be up.

For what it's worth, I am more than ever convinced that somebody killed Jamie, whether deliberately or by accident I don't know. Somebody in the local police, along with this Roberts man, fixed the evidence so as to get whoever did it off the hook and return a verdict of suicide – which they thought everybody would swallow after the stress of your prosecution. It's also possible that the same person was responsible for your arrest and conviction. I hope that you and Rob can go on to prove it.

I'm tired now – not used to all this writing – but I feel better for having put it all down. Now go get them, Paulie.

Your ever loving aunt

Meg.

I put the letter down and stared into space, trying to get my thoughts in order. Predominant in my mind was the sheer joy of knowing that Jamie had probably not broken his promise to me. Somehow I could cope with the idea that somebody might have been responsible for his death; it seemed stupid, I know, but it seemed possible that I would be able to mourn him properly now, the lovely boy that I had loved so much who'd had been taken from me.

Tears welled up again. My arms were resting on Rob's desk. I folded them, lay my head on them and wept for Jamie.

The Year of Awakening

Chapter 35

Josh

The taxi seemed to take for ever and the roads we were travelling on seemed to get narrower and narrower. It had been an odd day, full of sudden arrivals and departures, not least at my hotel in Skipton. I'd barely checked in and got to my room when Steve's text arrived so I'd had to go downstairs and check out again. They'd been very good about it but still charged me for the night, of course. I could hardly blame them.

The taxi arrived promptly. The driver was a chatty Asian guy who told me all about the area, in which he'd lived all his life. School contract runs regularly took him up to the district where Rob and Owen lived and he knew Owen as one of the local policemen. The journey was comfortable and friendly; it just seemed to take a bloody long time. I just wanted to get there, to be with Steve.

The cab's clock showed just after ten when we pulled into the drive of the converted farmhouse. I thanked the driver and paid him off with a good tip. Owen came out of the house to meet me and immediately took my bag. He quickly explained what was happening and that Steve was reading this letter from his aunt.

"If he's anything like Rob he'll be really upset by the letter, so be prepared."

Rob greeted me with a silent hug and showed me into the snug, where Steve was sitting, head on his arms, sobbing his heart out. God, it was a harrowing sight.

I moved quickly to his side and wrapped my arms round him. "Hey. Don't cry, Steve, I'm here now. Everything's going to be all right."

He lifted his head and immediately put his arms round my waist. I stood there and held him for a few minutes. His breathing slowed down and the sobbing stopped.

He lifted his head and looked at me. "He didn't kill himself, Josh. He didn't break his promise."

"So what happened?"

"It looks as if he was killed. Whether deliberately or by accident, we don't know."

"Christ, Steve."

"Now I can mourn him properly, let him go and maybe we can all get some peace at last."

He stood and took me in his arms properly, kissing me long and hard. "Thank you, Josh, for coming. I'm so grateful you're here."

I smiled up at him. "You can thank Barbara, too – she persuaded me that it was a good idea."

Rob stuck his head round the door. "Sorry to interrupt but I wondered whether we could have a family confab in a minute and whether Josh wanted any supper. There's loads of pasta left."

Even though I'd had a meal on the train earlier, his words

made me realise that I was hungry again, so I nodded enthusiastically. "Pasta sounds fantastic."

"And so does the conference," Steve added. "We'll be with you in a minute."

"Great. Owen's just going to crack a bottle of Chianti."

A few minutes later, I found myself at their kitchen table, devouring a huge plateful of pasta and sauce. With the wine as well, I was starting to feel human again. Steve was looking better too: he had some colour in his cheeks and a slight smile played round his lips.

Rob brought up the subject of his grandmother's letters first. "So, just to make sure we're on the same hymn sheet," he said, looking at Steve. "I assume Gran told you that she was convinced all along that Jamie didn't commit suicide and that the Roberts' investigation seemed to confirm that?"

Steve nodded. "She'd spoken to Derek Heath, who said that the file was with the CPS."

"Have there have been further developments since Meg's letter, Owen?" Steve asked.

"Yeah, I've been asking around at work," Owen replied. "It would seem that the CPS reckons they've got enough evidence to charge Roberts with perverting the course of justice in Jamie's case. The plan is to charge him with that next week. We understand that he's already confessed."

"And?" asked Steve.

"Roberts has named the policeman who asked him to fix the evidence. Apparently it was John Hardwick," Rob said.

"So that was why he was so keen to shut Meg up when she first raised the matter," Steve commented.

"Exactly," Owen interjected. "He and Roberts must have known that their evidence wouldn't stand intensive scrutiny so they wanted to keep the case closed and forgotten about."

"Where does that leave Jamie, then?" Steve asked.

"The detectives are still not sure whether it was murder or manslaughter and they have no firm idea who was responsible. John Hardwick died last year, so they can't question him but they're going to talk to his son Ned soon. That might bring something to light."

"But if it was only an accident, why would Ned's father have felt the need to cover it up?" I asked.

"Good point, Josh," Owen responded. "That's why they think the killing may well have been deliberate."

"Christ, what a mess," said Steve. He turned to Rob. "I think you and I had better have a chat with Derek Heath fairly soon."

Rob nodded. "I'll ring him in the morning. He may well be coming to the funeral anyway."

"Then I think we'd better call it a night," Steve said, standing up and stretching. "Tomorrow will be a bit of a roller coaster."

"You're not kidding," Owen responded with a grimace, gathering up our glasses.

Steve and I said our goodnights and went to the guest room. Once there, I found myself wrapped in Steve's arms.

He hugged me tightly for a few moments without speaking then whispered in my ear. "I'm so glad you're here, Josh. Thank you."

I tilted my head back slightly to look into his eyes. There was still some sign of the redness caused by his earlier distress. "Well, somebody's got to keep an eye on you. You've been on your own for too long, Steve. It's about time you had somebody at your back."

He smiled and kissed me gently on the lips. "Well I'm glad it's you because you give the most awesome cuddles."

I laughed. "We aim to please. So let's get ready for bed so that normal cuddling service can be resumed."

"That sounds like a plan," Steve responded.

And so it was that we settled down, snuggled together, ready to face whatever tomorrow would bring.

The Year of Awakening

Chapter 36

Steve

It was not long after six when I awoke, still wrapped in Josh's embrace. It was warm and comforting and I was reluctant to move, but I needed the bathroom so I disentangled myself as gently as possible and got out of bed. Sunshine was streaming through a large dormer window set into the roof. After I relieved myself, I went over to look at the view.

It was glorious. Because I'd arrived at dusk, I didn't realise how high we had climbed. The house was set on a ridge above the surrounding countryside. I could see Ingleborough to the right and then a 180-degree panorama of dales and hills, with the mountains of the Lake District in the far distance behind them. There was a virtually cloudless blue sky and the air was crystal clear, so that the view was pin sharp. Magnificent.

The view across London from my place was pretty special but it had nothing on this. God, what had I been missing by not coming back here for more than twenty years? Would last night's revelations mean that I would feel able to come again for pleasure rather than duty? I hoped so.

Josh was still dead to the world and looked so incredibly beautiful, his chestnut hair contrasting with the white of the pillow. I smiled. There was this lovely, lovely man, and he loved *me*. How incredible was that? If the last twenty-one years of loneliness had been a preparation for this, then they were worth it.

I smiled and shook my head as if to clear it. There were sounds of movement in the house and a dog barked. The odour of frying bacon drifted into the room. Enough of introspection – it was time to go and face the day.

After breakfast, Rob spoke to the solicitor, Derek Heath. He was planning to come to the funeral and would have a chat with us afterwards. Owen had words with colleagues in Skipton, who confirmed that they planned to question Hardwick's son later that day.

Meanwhile there was the funeral itself to get through. Rob had arranged for a service in the village church, followed by a private interment in a sustainable burial ground across the valley. Afterwards, there would be a wake in Meg's local, the White Horse, one of the two pubs in the village. Owen would drive from their house to the White Horse, park there and meet us at the church. Rob and I would ride to the church in the undertaker's limousine. I asked if Josh could accompany me. We would follow the hearse from Settle through to Long Garfield.

I knew that the day would be a bit like an obstacle course – a series of reminders of my childhood and teenage years, of Jamie and my parents, as well as the aunt we were there to mourn. Not that any of the memories were bad in themselves; it was just that the night of my arrest and its sequel lay across my history like a deep scar which had yet to heal properly. Revisiting the scene of those events twenty-one years ago was likely to reopen the wound.

The funeral car was scheduled for eleven. The four of us had a leisurely breakfast before getting changed into our formal clothes. As Josh and I got ready, we were quiet. I could see the concern in his eyes.

"Are you okay, Steve?"

"Yeah, fine at the moment. Seeing the village again is going to be difficult, though. And I'm nervous about seeing loads of people from my childhood. I can't say I'm looking forward to it."

"No, I can understand that. Still, we'll manage, I'm sure – and don't worry if you need me to fade into the background. I'm here for you, not anybody else, so we can be out and proud or modest and discreet, or I can just be a random stranger. Whatever you feel comfortable with."

"Thanks, Josh, that's really helpful. I must admit I hadn't given it any thought. I suppose with Rob and Owen being out locally, having us there as another couple won't be a problem."

Josh shrugged. "Whatever. I just wanted you to know that you're not to worry about me. I shan't be upset however it plays out."

"Thanks. And thanks for being here." I pulled him into a hug, as ever relishing the comfort of his arms.

"Car's here!" Rob's voice cut across our moment of reverie, so we picked up our jackets and headed out of the door.

The Dales weather was being uncharacteristically kind that day. We left the house and travelled to the village in glorious sunshine, though the wind was sharp. We rode through the narrow lanes before crossing the bypass and going into Settle, where we met the hearse and proceeded in a solemn procession into Long Garfield.

The sight of the village immediately gave me a lump in my throat. Obviously, it had changed in the last twenty years, but not radically. It was still tucked into a shoulder of the hills that surrounded it on three sides. On the fourth side, the ground sloped away towards the river.

It was, if anything, a bit tidier than I remembered. There were new houses on a couple of agricultural sites and one or two more barns had been converted. But the street pattern and the personality of the place were unaltered. The stone of the buildings gave a sense of permanence, as if the houses had grown fully formed from the limestone of the hills. The dark of their slate roofs added to the sense of organic growth.

We went through the village on our way up to the church, passing my childhood home. Ahead, just on the right, was Jamie's family home, where he and I had had such happy times. But it had also been the scene of my arrest and the start of the downward spiral of those terrible few months. My eyes began to sting and I let out a long sigh. Josh was evidently watching because he reached out and took my hand. I squeezed his fingers and then held on for dear life.

We turned off the main road by the White Horse and headed up the lane towards the church. As we drew up outside, I could see a knot of people at the door, including

Owen. He came and joined us as we waited for them to extract the coffin from the hearse. Then we were ready to process into the building. As we began to move, I noticed with a small smile that Rob reached for Owen's hand. I did the same once more with Josh.

The church was full as the people of the village and the wider area gathered to pay their respects to a much-loved resident who had, without doubt, been a 'character'.

Rob had prepared for the funeral very carefully and was determined to pay personal tribute to his grandmother despite Owen's concern that he might be too upset to speak. As he rose to address the congregation and turned to face them, it must have dawned on him just how many people were there. His eyes opened wide and he gave a small gasp. I thought for a moment that he might bolt, but he gathered himself together and started to speak.

After describing Meg's birth in the village in 1933, he went on to talk about her marriage to his grandfather, who was a local farmer. Her upbringing had conditioned her to a life as a farmer's wife, to marrying and bringing up a family of her own. And a farmer's wife she duly became, marrying Rob's grandfather, George, in Coronation Year.

No children had come though; Meg had channelled her energy into village affairs instead, becoming a member of the parish council and then the rural district council. Then, after Meg and George had almost given up hope, their son Bill was born in 1963. He joined his father on the farm and married his childhood sweetheart Angie, Rob's mother, in 1981. Meg had become a grandmother two years later; she had called Rob her 'bundle of joy'.

But the joy was short-lived and her life had careered

off its path after George died of a heart attack in 1987. A year later, Rob's parents were killed in an accident on the A65. The farm had to be sold so that Meg and six-year-old Rob moved into a small cottage in the village, the house in which she lived for the rest of her life.

After a while, Meg resumed her political career and became a county councillor, only standing down when she reached the age of seventy-five. She had remained a member of the parish council, though, and consequently was well-known in the village to people of all generations.

"As you know, my grandmother stood no more than four foot nine in her stockinged feet, and was feisty, outspoken and opinionated. I loved every inch of her, even though she made my life hell at times," Rob continued, his emotion reflected in his voice. "I shall miss you, gran."

I was immensely moved by Rob's tribute and recalled my own experience of her. She had understood my refusal to come anywhere near Long Garfield when I left prison, but she had kept in touch, visiting me regularly in London when she was on county council business. She had pushed me hard to complete my degree and follow my dream to help with the environment, a subject close to her own heart.

In the silence that followed Rob's words, I bowed my head to hide the tears that welled up. Josh sensed my distress and squeezed my hand.

Suddenly, there was a small commotion at the back of the church. I looked round in time to see a latecomer take his place in the back row. He was a man of roughly my own age, heavily built and shabbily dressed in an old waxed jacket. He was red in the face and clearly short of breath.

He looked round defiantly, as if knowing that he was not welcome at the service but was determined to be here anyway. He met my eye briefly and I saw his expression change. He narrowed his eyes and his face took on a look of such malevolence that I almost recoiled physically. Suddenly, I knew who it was.

Ned Hardwick.

Ned Hardwick. My God. I'd not thought of him for over twenty years. A big, scruffy bear of a boy, he'd been a classmate of Jamie's at junior school. I seemed to remember Jamie saying that they were quite good friends at one stage.

But then the eleven-plus exam had divided them. Ned had not passed so had gone to secondary school in Settle, rather than to the grammar school like Jamie and me.

Ned Hardwick, who'd made Jamie's life a misery by effectively stalking him for two years. He said he still wanted to be friends but claimed that Jamie had pushed him away. "You're too posh now and wouldn't be seen with the likes of me," he'd said. In fact, life at the grammar school was demanding and didn't leave much time for hanging round the bus shelter or the playground doing not a lot. Besides, Jamie had met me on the bus by then and our friendship meant that he had no time at all for his former friend.

Instead, Ned formed his own small gang from his mates at the high school. They became the village bullies. They chased and intimidated younger kids and generally caused trouble – minor acts of vandalism, making sarcastic remarks about local people, hanging out together in the village at night. But Ned kept a special place in his malicious heart for Jamie, following him and chanting names, threatening him and trying to steal his school bag on the way home from the bus.

Being an older boy and strongly built, I was able to intervene on a couple of occasions, so I was quickly added to his list of hate targets. And, of course, he was the local copper's son so thought himself to be – and in practice was – invulnerable and beyond discipline or punishment.

I remembered now that my Auntie Meg was the only person who was prepared to act; she was the one who brought his reign of terror to an end. After one particular incident in which a pensioner had been jostled and had fallen, she marched round to the Hardwick household and tore a strip off both father and son. She threatened to report the episode to the chief constable and all sorts of other dire consequences.

Ned was grounded for a few weeks and lost face with his gang. He was never the same boy again, turning in on himself and becoming surly and resentful. I knew that Jamie was still wary of Ned. We used to come across him in the oddest of places when we were out together, almost as if he was following us or spying on us.

Judging by the look on his face that afternoon at Meg's funeral, he remembered all that as clearly as I did. Suddenly, standing in that church, everything clicked into place. Of course! Ned had been the one responsible for my arrest and imprisonment, directing his father's attention to Jamie and me. I also suspected, with some certainty, that Ned had been involved in Jamie's death.

I shivered. Josh felt the movement and shot me a questioning look.

"Tell you later," I whispered and turned my full attention back to my aunt's funeral service. A final hymn was followed by the blessing and the service ended. Rob and I followed the coffin from the church and took our places at the door to greet Meg's friends and neighbours as they emerged. We were followed out by Owen and Josh, who stood quietly to one side.

The process of greeting everybody was hard, especially since there were several older villagers who remembered me as a boy and wanted to say hello. They were very kind, leaving me with an odd feeling; the warmth of their greeting was cheering but added to the burden I felt from coming home. I promised several of them a longer chat later at the White Horse.

At one point, I remembered to look round for Ned Hardwick. I checked with Rob but it seemed that Ned had left the church ahead of the coffin and been seen heading across the fields to his home.

It took around twenty minutes to greet everybody from the full church, then we had to assemble for the short drive to the burial ground on the other side of the valley. There were just the four of us and the vicar, standing at the graveside, our hair blowing in a stiff south-westerly breeze. It was a beautiful place, with views over the three peaks of Ingleborough, Whernside and Pen-y-ghent, and a clear view of the River Ribble as it meandered through the valley. You could do worse, I reflected, than to end your days in such a spot.

The vicar read the words of the burial service in the

original seventeenth-century form and, as their authors intended, they found their mark.

> MAN that is born of a woman hath but a short time to live, and is full of misery. He cometh up, and is cut down, like a flower; he fleeth as it were a shadow, and never continueth in one stay.
>
> In the midst of life we are in death: of whom may we seek for succour, but of thee, O Lord, who for our sins art justly displeased?

It was certainly true that Jamie had been cut down like a flower and that my life after his death had been full of misery. There had been nobody from whom to seek succour, save the woman we were now burying.

Then I smiled to myself: Meg's life had certainly not been full of misery. Challenges, certainly. Periods of heartache, definitely. But she'd had the blessing of Bill's birth and a fascinating life, in which she'd had the satisfaction of helping others.

> FORASMUCH as it hath pleased Almighty God of his great mercy to take unto himself the soul of our dear sister here departed: we therefore commit her body to the ground; earth to earth, ashes to ashes, dust to dust; in sure and certain hope of the Resurrection to eternal life, through our Lord Jesus Christ...

Well, up to a point. Try as I might, I had never managed to achieve the leap of faith that would make me a true believer in the resurrection and eternal life, any more than Auntie Meg had been. But I did know that Meg would live on in our memories as the feisty, opinionated campaigner she had been all her life – and that those memories would be shared with others in the village and handed on to others through the work she had done and the benefits she had obtained for her fellow citizens.

But the fact was that we would never hear her voice again, nor be on the receiving end of one her penetrating stares. Nor laugh with her over dinner and a bottle of wine. The thought saddened me as her coffin was lowered into the ground. Rob stepped forward to sprinkle earth on the coffin and I followed. I stepped back and reached once more for Josh's hand. The contact grounded me again and my moment of sadness passed. It had been a job well done, this funeral. We would remember Meg as a formidable woman who was nevertheless a kindly soul, looking out for others throughout her long life. That was not a bad epitaph for anybody, I felt, and our remembrance of her represented at least some form of an afterlife.

We turned from the graveside and walked back to the car. It was time for the wake, to join the villagers in marking Meg's passing at the White Horse.

The Year of Awakening

Chapter 37

Josh

Steve maintained an outward appearance of composure throughout the funeral service and the interment. There were two signs of the emotional strain he was under: the firm, not to say rigid, set of his jaw, and the fact that he held my hand at every available opportunity. It was as if he was using me as some sort of earth, discharging his negative energy through me.

I was more than happy to do whatever was necessary to get him through the day and away from the village later that afternoon. I could only begin to imagine what he must be feeling at coming back here after so many years – and at a time when he could only store up more unhappy memories.

As we got back into the official car after the burial, both Rob and Steve seemed to fold like wet cardboard.

"Well done, boys," said Owen. "You both did really well there. So hard, I know, but you came through with flying colours."

Rob grinned at his husband. "Thanks, man. I almost lost

it a couple of times, especially during the speech."

"Yeah, you did really well, Rob," I chimed in. "It was really touching."

"Meg would have been proud of you," said Steve.

"Thanks," Rob replied with a grin. "I was determined to do it, but when I stood up and saw the church so full, I nearly passed out. I had no idea that many people would turn up."

"So what's the form now?" Steve asked.

"At the White Horse? Well, I've arranged for drinks to be served when we get there – one free for everybody. Then they'll serve a buffet lunch followed by tea and coffee. Obviously anybody can buy more drinks if they want to. Judging by previous funerals I've been to, pretty much everybody will be gone by half three or four. We'll have plenty of time to pick up your stuff and get you to the station by six."

"Fine," Steve responded. Then there was a pause. "Oh, by the way, did you see that bloke come into the church late?"

"The one who made a bit of a commotion?" asked Owen. "That was our friend Ned Hardwick."

"Hmm. Thought I recognised him. He was in Jamie's class at the village school, you know. Funny bloke. Couldn't ever forgive Jamie for passing his eleven plus. Was a very troubled teenager, as I recall."

"So not much has changed then," replied Owen with a grin. "String of convictions as long as your arm. Domestic abuse, actual bodily harm, drunk and disorderly – you name it, he's been in court for it."

"Any idea why?"

Owen shook his head. "He just seems to be terminally angry – that's the only way I can put it. When he was still alive, his father used to despair of him. He couldn't understand where all his aggression came from."

"It is odd," Steve replied. "His mother was the most placid of women, I seem to remember, and I don't think his father was particularly volatile."

"Not really," Owen said. "He did have a temper on him at the time I arrived here. But, of course, that might have been his illness starting. Formidable when roused sums it up quite well, I think."

"What did the father die of?" Josh asked.

"Brain tumour," Rob told him. "Quite sudden, Gran said. Diagnosed in the April, dead by September."

"Gosh," Steve breathed. "That quick, eh? Makes you think."

"Quite," Owen responded. "Ned didn't cope very well, I'm afraid. It's around then that he got into his biggest trouble."

"Poor man," I said.

"Possibly," Owen remarked. "Though you might not say that if you were at the other end of his formidable right hook."

We all laughed. Eventually, it was Steve who spoke again. "Seriously, though, guys. I think he's dangerous. The look he gave me when he recognised me in church was really poisonous. We need to watch it if he turns up at the White Horse."

"Oh, he'll be there all right," said Owen. "He practically lives there. It drives Ann and Gerry mad."

Steve looked at Owen with amazement. "Ann and

Gerry? Are they really still the landlords?"

"Yup. They'll have been there twenty-nine years come September," Rob told me.

"That's amazing!" Steve responded. "God, I can remember Gerry serving me my first legal pint!"

"And a few illegal ones before that, I've no doubt," grumbled Owen.

"No comment, officer!"

"Me neither," Rob added with a laugh.

By this time, we had reached the village once more and the car pulled up outside the White Horse. It looked friendly and welcoming – a true traditional village pub. I looked across at Steve and noticed him wince again, as if in pain. Another memory, I guessed.

I squeezed his hand and he looked up at me, giving me the briefest of nods and a small smile as if to say 'I can do this'. I hoped he was right.

Chapter 37

Steve

Pulling up outside the White Horse prompted more nostalgia and a stab of pain as I remembered that the last time I'd been in there was the last evening that Jamie and I spent together before my arrest. My parents, Jamie's parents, Jamie and I had come for a post-Christmas supper. The place had been packed and there'd been live music – a pianist, I seemed to remember. We'd all had a great time; it had been one of those nights where closing time simply meant closing the curtains very tightly. Ann and Gerry had always known how to turn an ordinary night into a great party.

I must have shown the pain that the sudden memory brought because I saw Josh looking at me with concern and felt him squeeze my hand. I took a deep breath and nodded and smiled at him, offering reassurance that I could do this.

I was prepared for the White Horse to have changed in the twenty-one years since I had last crossed its threshold. I didn't know what to expect but, after all, times changed, particularly in the pub business. What I was not prepared for was that it was still exactly the same. Other than a coat of fresh emulsion on the walls and the names on the beer pumps, I was walking into the space we had left that night in 1992.

Tears sprang to my eyes. It felt really uncanny as I walked into the main room and looked across the bar to the snug beyond, what might have been known as the public bar in the old days, home to the dartboard and domino tables, uncarpeted and therefore available to walkers, cyclists and local workers who were shod in boots and such like. The piano still stood in the corner of the main room, tucked in just by the door into the dining room.

This lay to the right of the main room, and all three spaces were heated by old-fashioned coal fires in the winter, which made the place cosy. Other guests who had been at the funeral service had gone straight from church to pub, so were already ensconced, drinks in hand.

We were greeted warmly and, having obtained our drinks, the four of us were quickly split up into separate discussions around the pub. There was a buzz of conversation and somewhere across the room, somebody let out a guffaw of laughter. It seemed set fair to turn into another White Horse 'occasion', entirely fitting to celebrate Meg's life. She had been a regular who liked nothing better than a good drink and a good gossip, not to mention a good sing-song when the occasion arose.

Rob gave a short speech of welcome to everybody before the buffet was served, a magnificent spread laid out in the dining room. He also introduced me, much to my embarrassment, saying how good it was to see me back in the village after so many years.

People started to make their way to the food. I was about to follow when I heard a female voice calling my former name from the snug. "Paul? Paul Bates, is it really you?"

I turned round, not knowing who to expect. I smiled and said, "Actually it's Steve Frazer now, but it's still me." For a moment, I was puzzled about the identity of this stranger and then she smiled, her eyes narrowing with the skin either side crinkling up. I recognised her immediately, even though it was so long since I had last seen her. The look she gave me was exactly the same as I'd seen on the day we met, nigh on thirty-seven years earlier, at our first day at infant school.

Maggie Grayson. My best friend and constant companion at the village school for more than six years, and a close friend to both Jamie and me throughout our relationship. As I had gone to university in Leeds, she'd gone off to London to study music. I had not seen her since just before my arrest.

"Maggie Grayson." I smiled. "Well I never...'

I found myself locked into a big hug. "Paul, Steve, whatever. It's so great to see you again after all this time. How long is it? Must be more than twenty years."

"Yep," I replied. "Christmas Eve, 1992. In this very bar."

Maggie's face fell. "Just before...'

"Quite."

"I was so sorry about all that, my love. It must have been so terrible for you."

I nodded, unable to speak for a moment or two. It was another of those occasions which brought the whole experience back to me in sharp relief. I took a deep breath and swallowed hard before smiling back at her. "Still a bit difficult, even after all this time. Especially today... it's my first time back in the village since. Couldn't miss Meg's funeral, though."

Maggie looked horrified. "Sorry. I mean sorry that it all happened, obviously, and that it's still so raw for you. But I'm also sorry about Meg. We only moved into the village three months ago and she gave us a great welcome."

"So who's 'we', then?"

"Oh, sorry! Of course, you don't know. But then again why would you? Sorry, I'm burbling. 'We' equals Diane and I plus two dogs and a cat. Diane is my wife. She's a music producer specialising in jazz. We met at college and got together about fifteen years ago. We finally did our CP four years ago."

"Gosh!" I said. "Well, good for you. What brought you back to Long Garfield then?"

"To cut a long story short, we were both fed up with the rat race. Diane recently went freelance and can now work from anywhere. We worked out that if she wanted her own studio, which she did, we had to get out of London. There was just no way we'd be able to afford anywhere large enough to put one in, much less buy all the gear. So we started looking and then I saw this barn conversion for sale right in the centre of the village. It was perfect – and the fact that it was in the village in which I was born was an added bonus."

"Sounds fantastic," I responded. "Is Diane here? I'd love to meet her."

Maggie shook her head. "Unfortunately, she had a client

meeting today in Leeds which she couldn't get out of. She said she'd try to get back in time to raise a glass to Meg if she could, though."

"Oh, shame. Another time, perhaps."

"And what about you?" she asked. "Did you finish your degree? What are you doing now?"

"I took an Open University degree a couple of years after … everything. I ended up as an environmental consultant," I responded. "Three of us set up in business together a few years ago. We operate from offices in South London – Crystal Palace to be exact. I live about three minutes' walk from the office. It's my ideal commute."

She laughed. "I can imagine. And did I see you with a rather nice-looking boy at the service?"

"Yeah. That's Josh. Joined the firm a few months ago and was daft enough to decide that he wanted to be my boyfriend." I let out a short bark of laughter. "Still can't believe it, really."

"He's certainly very good looking."

"Yes, he's certainly that," I replied, a little defensively. "But he's also funny, kind, unbelievably patient, and a bloody good consultant. Oh, and Diane might be interested in the fact that he's an absolutely fantastic jazz pianist. Like I say, I still can't believe my luck in meeting him."

As if on cue, we heard the first notes of a tune strike up on the pub's ancient upright piano. I looked across into the other bar to catch sight of the famous chestnut curls bobbing away as he struck up 'Fly Me to the Moon' again.

The Year of Awakening

Chapter 38

Josh

As soon as we reached the pub, Owen took me under his wing. I was very grateful; I knew nobody there and nobody knew me either. I could have stuck with Steve, forcing him to introduce me to everybody as his boyfriend – but I felt that was just too complicated, especially today of all days when the focus should be on his aunt.

Owen understood this instinctively; he was in something of a similar position today. Even though he was widely known and recognised as one of the local bobbies, he had no status at this event but he wanted to be around to support Rob when he needed it. So we settled into a corner of the main room.

It gave me an opportunity look round and take in my surroundings. I was impressed. The warmth of the atmosphere in the place was obvious and people were chatting away to each other, most of them sharing their favourite reminiscences about Meg. She certainly sounded to be a character and I rather wished that I had known her.

"So how did you get on with Meg?" I asked Owen.

"Oh, really well," he replied. "She was very kind to me and always welcoming whenever I called. And when we decided to do our CP, she was amazing. Rob said that she always was one for a party, right from when he was little. And boy, did we have one that day!"

"Were you in here?" I asked.

Owen grinned. "We certainly were. We did the ceremony in the Registry Office about eleven-thirty and then came on here. I think Rob and I finally rolled out of here and up the road to Meg's around nine-thirty that night. I remember it well, even though Rob and I were so drunk that the only way we managed to get home was to hold each other up. You should have seen us tottering up the street leaning against one another."

"Amazing," I laughed, feeling more relaxed than at any time during this rather bizarre day.

"So, Owen," said a female voice. "Aren't you going to introduce us to this rather lovely young man?"

I looked round to see a couple of elderly ladies standing there with big smiles on their faces. Owen grinned back at them. "But of course. Annie and Sheila, can I present Josh Ashcroft? Josh, this is Annie Trueman and Sheila Lorrimer." He paused, before adding in explanation, "These two were Meg's boozing pals and sparring partners."

"How very nice to meet you ladies," I replied with my best smile. "I was just thinking earlier how much I would like to have known Meg."

"You didn't get to meet her, then?" asked Annie.

"No, I didn't meet Steve until a few months ago when I joined his firm," I said. "We've only been dating a few weeks."

"You seem much younger than him," Sheila interjected.

I felt Owen shift uncomfortably in his seat but I kept smiling. "I've always had an eye for a good vintage when I see one. Besides, I'm perhaps older than I look. I've always found low lighting very flattering, you know, and it's quite dim in here."

"Well, I hope you're looking after Steve properly," said Annie with mock severity. "He was very precious to Meg and we all need to look out for him now she's gone."

I nodded vigorously. "You can rely on me, ladies. Believe me, he's very special to me too."

"And you really mean that," whispered Sheila. "I can tell."

I nodded again, adding in my cod southern accent, "Sure did, ma'am. Every darned word of it. So what did you ladies and Meg used to get up to together? Did you go and spot the local talent in Skipton?"

They giggled at that. "No, no," Sheila explained. "Nothing like that at our age ... unfortunately," she added with a giggle. "No, we used to come in here most nights and annoy the hell out of Anne and Gerry."

Owen chipped in. "The three of them are wicked dominoes players," he said. "And these two throw a mean dart as well."

"Not forgetting our sing-songs!" Annie interjected.

"Sing-songs?" I asked.

"Yes, we have a regular pianist who comes in a couple of times a month. There's nothing like gathering round the piano and singing your heart out."

I laughed, "You won't find me disagreeing with you

there. I love playing for a pub full of people singing."

The two old ladies' eyes lit up. "You play the piano?" they asked, more or less in unison.

"Yep."

"So would you play for us now?"

"Well ... do you think it would be appropriate?" I queried. "This is a funeral, after all."

"That was earlier," countered Sheila. "This is now a party to celebrate Meg's life. And there was nothing she loved more than somebody playing that piano."

"I'll just clear it with Rob," said Owen, disappearing briefly.

Annie's face took on a serious expression for a moment. "Josh, you know about the history of Steve and this place, don't you?"

I nodded. "Yeah, Steve told me the whole sad story a few weeks ago. I was horrified."

"He's had a tough time ever since. That was why Meg was so protective of him."

"I can well understand," I countered with a big smile. "Trust me, ladies. I've got his back."

Just then Owen returned, grinning from ear to ear. "Rob says that the ladies are right. Meg would have loved to think that we had a good old sing-song at her last party."

I went over to the instrument and lifted the lid. Gerry, the landlord, was there, and gave me a nod of approval. I ran my fingers over the keys to get a feel for the instrument and then began to play. It struck me that the best thing to do was to use my open-mike night programme to kick things off and then see where it went.

I had a sudden thought. "Owen, can you find out what

Meg's favourite tunes were?"

I started the introduction of 'Fly Me to the Moon' and started to sing. I was suddenly aware of the whole room falling silent, just like the pub in Lewisham the previous week. It was an amazing feeling.

The Year of Awakening

Chapter 39

Steve

As had happened in London the previous week, the whole room quietened as Josh began to sing. Once again his rich baritone voice dominated the whole pub. It was astonishing; some people literally stopped speaking in mid-sentence and held their mouths open, as if struck dumb by some sort of magic spell.

Somewhere to my left, one of the exterior doors opened and a strikingly tall, attractive woman entered the room. She saw Maggie next to me and smiled at her. This must be Diane, I thought, as I saw her stand stock still and listen to the music coming from the other bar. Pleasure and amazement were clearly visible on her face, too.

Josh's first number came to an end to riotous applause. I reckoned that I knew what was coming next. I was not sure that I'd be able to listen to 'Someone to Watch Over Me' in this room in this pub. As the opening chords of the song began, you could hear a pin drop in the pub.

I prepared to move towards the back door to get some air, but Maggie must have seen something in my expression because she reached out and squeezed my hand, forestalling my attempts to move.

As I had known it would, the poignancy of the lyrics and the sound of Josh's voice unleashed the emotions I'd held in all day about Meg, about Jamie, and all that had happened during that winter. The tears coursed down my cheeks and I had to let at least one sob escape me. I felt a hand at my back and looked up to see my cousin Rob standing close, looking at me with concern. His eyes weren't dry either.

"Gran loved this song," he whispered to me. I nodded and smiled, recovering myself a little as I did so. "Josh has got a fantastic voice, Steve. It's stunning." Again, I nodded.

As Josh reached the final phrase, the room erupted. It transformed my mood and a big grin replaced my tears. I was so proud of him for helping to make my aunt's funeral day so memorable for all of us.

Rob noticed the change and nodded. "That's better," he whispered.

The applause died down, and I heard the chords of Josh's favourite, "Luck Be A Lady'. Once again, the room fell silent as he sang.

It was clear that Josh could have had a job for life playing all the audience's requests, and I marvelled at his knowledge of the repertoire. Since he had no music with him, everything he played and sang had to be from memory.

But time was getting on. I glanced at my watch and

realised that we would have to leave soon if we were to catch our train home. Owen had obviously had the same thought since I noticed him say something into Josh's ear. He nodded, and at the end of the song announced that the next would have to be his last number. As he gave the title, he looked round the room until he caught sight of me in the doorway of the snug. He grinned as he struck up another tune from *Guys and Dolls*, 'I'll Know When My Love Comes Along'.

As the song drew to a close, there was a bit of a kerfuffle by the street door into the snug and a figure forced its way into the still-crowded room. I looked up to identify the source of the disturbance and found myself looking into the hate-filled eyes of Ned Hardwick for the second time that day.

After a moment or two, he looked away and pushed through the crowd towards the bar. As he drew level with me, he looked up again. "You got a problem with me being here, queer boy?"

"None whatever, Ned," I replied evenly. "It's a free country, even for people like me. So have *you* got a problem?"

"Yeah, actually," he replied. "I don't like you being back in the village – you and your fancy boyfriend, and your queer cousin as well."

The music had stopped in the other room and there were audible gasps from the people in the snug. Rob moved to stand by my side once more and Owen appeared in the doorway between the snug and the main bar.

Undeterred, Ned continued. "Seems to me that the village has been a better place for the last twenty-odd years without you in it."

What the fuck? What had I done to deserve this tirade?

I was striving to remain calm but, with all that Rob, Owen, Josh and I had talked about last night about Ned and his father, I wasn't about to let him get away with that crap. Gerry was trying to intervene, to get me to back off, but I was having none of it.

"And why would that be then, Ned?"

"One less fucking queer hanging around, corrupting people like you corrupted Jamie. You went to jail for that, didn't you, queer boy? Always seemed to me that they let you out too fucking early. Me, I'd have left you to rot in there."

When the conversation started I had been known it might get nasty, but not this nasty. I started to tremble with anger. Owen moved towards Ned but I waved him off.

I tried to keep my voice reasonable. "Ned, you know that Jamie and I were in love, that it was a consensual relationship which we'd told our parents about. You must know that because you watched us often enough, didn't you?"

His eyes blazed and he balled his fists. "You fucking stole Jamie from me. He was *my* friend at school here. It was only when he went to that fucking posh fucking school down the road that I lost him. After that it was all 'Paul Bates this and Paul Bates that. He's my friend now.' God I fucking *hate* you."

He paused and moved a step closer. Owen did the same. Then Ned grinned wickedly and spoke again. "And then you started screwing him, didn't you? Yeah, I used to watch you, follow you to all your secret places. And you knew I was there, didn't you? Spoiling the fun, scaring you both. When you both came out, it was more difficult – you could stay at home and do it. Well, I fucking put a stop to that in the end, didn't I? Got you sent to jail, my dad and I, didn't we? Dad made sure that you got a good long prison sentence – helps, being pals with the magistrate. God, I enjoyed that day. I was so fucking pleased, seeing you go down those steps in court. Doing your little-boy-lost bit, weren't you, you fucking cunt. Not the clever-arse grammar school boy then, were you? Just another pervert, going to jail where you fucking belonged."

I was desperately trying to keep my temper but it was bloody difficult. I'd never throughout my life known what it was like to be hated – really *hated* – by somebody. But I was sure as hell finding out now, and it was terrifying listening to the unadulterated malice in his voice.

I longed to strike him – to shut his filthy mouth with my fists. But I couldn't, not yet at least. I'd solved one mystery tonight and my gut instinct told me that I was about to solve another. I just had to hold my nerve for a few minutes longer... And now I saw my way.

"So what did you do when I was out of the way, Ned? Did you go round and claim your friend back? I bet he was really fucking pleased to see you."

He flinched at that and I felt a thrill. I knew I was on the right lines. He took another step forward so that we were only four feet or so apart.

"What did you want to do to him, Ned? Try to take my place? Was that your idea? Because I don't think he would have liked that. In fact he didn't, did he? What did he do,

Ned, when you asked him? Did he tell you to sling your hook? You can't play the innocent with me, Ned Hardwick – I know. You hated me not because you disapproved but because you were jealous, weren't you? You wanted to do it instead, didn't you, Ned? You really wanted to be a queer boy just like Jamie and me. But Daddy wouldn't let you, would he?

He flinched again. I was definitely on to something.

"And what did you do when Jamie rejected you, Ned? Did you bash his head in first and then drown him in the beck? Or did you just throw him in the beck so that he hit his head on his way into the water? Because you were there, weren't you, Ned? You saw Jamie die, didn't you? He wasn't going to be your friend again so he had to die, didn't he?"

I saw the panic in his eyes. *Bingo!*

My instincts had been right. Of course, there was no evidence to put Ned at the scene. Everybody now accepted that Jamie's death was definitely not suicide, despite the evidence being fixed by that man Russell and Ned's father, but that was as far as it went. But logic dictated that if Jamie hadn't killed himself then this man was involved. I needed to goad him into an admission.

There was panic in Ned's voice when he spoke again. "I didn't do it deliberately! I didn't mean him to die. He shouldn't have started to cry. When I told him what I'd done, how I'd done it for us, him and me, so that we could be friends like we had been before *you,* he just burst into tears. I couldn't fucking stand that. I wanted to make him stop, to tell him that it would be all right, I'd look after him now. But he backed away from me and then he began to fall backwards into the water. I reached out to grab him, but it was too late. I heard the noise he made as his head hit a stone. I knew there was a problem, that it was serious. But it was an accident, you have to believe me." This last was not addressed to me but to the room as a whole as he looked from one shocked face to another.

I saw tears gather in his eyes and I knew I'd won. I'd found out what really happened that January day in 1993. Suddenly, Ned looked like a defeated man – but if I thought the confrontation was over, I had another think coming.

He realised that he'd been trapped into the admission and began to seek a way out. Now he had nothing to lose. He dashed the tears from his eyes with clenched fists and stood straight again. His eyes filled with hate again as they sought mine. Then he spoke, reaching inside his coat at the same time. "I didn't kill Jamie deliberately. But you, on the other hand, you fucking bastard..."

In three seconds, it was all over. He took two steps towards me and removed his hand from his coat. I noticed a flash of steel in his right hand then felt a sharp pain in the gut. Then everything went black.

The Year of Awakening

Chapter 40

Josh

I heard the commotion start in the snug as I finished my last song. Owen had reminded me that it was almost time for us to leave and, truth to tell, I was rather glad. I'd been playing and singing solidly for over an hour – way longer than I had ever done before – and this was on top of everything else that had happened today. I was definitely starting to fade.

Then the shouting started and the pub fell quiet. I heard Steve's voice and immediately feared one of his meltdowns. I stood up from the piano stool and forced my way through the people to the door into the snug. Owen was there and I stood next to him, peering round his shoulder into the room. I saw Steve and another man facing each other. Steve had his back to me so it was difficult to see what was going on, but I could tell by his voice that he was in control of himself.

The tone, the abuse and the language were awful and some of Ned's barbs made me flinch. But I could see what Steve was trying to do.

Then it happened. I didn't see the knife because Ned's body was shielded, but I saw Steve double up and pass out. All hell let loose. Several women screamed. Owen rushed forward to grab Ned, pinning his arms to his side and then wrestling him to the floor. Rob, who had been standing immediately behind Steve, grabbed him to prevent him from falling. I leapt into the room and helped Rob to support Steve. Between us we lowered him to the floor so that we could see the extent of his wound and try to stop any bleeding.

"Ambulance, please!" I yelled. "Can somebody please call an ambulance?"

Gerry shouted, "I'm onto to it!" The other bar staff, under instruction from Owen, tried to move everybody away from Steve and out of the snug.

"Rob, if he's bleeding, put pressure on the wound to try and stop it," Owen called out.

We complied immediately. Steve was definitely still alive and breathing reasonably well, but he was still out cold. As I looked down, the full force of what had happened and the possible consequences struck me like a high-speed train. I went cold at the thought that we might lose him and I felt the sting of tears at the back of my eyes.

"Come on, Steve," I breathed as I stroked his face. "Hold on. Help's on its way. We'll get you to hospital. It's going to be all right. We've got you." I was talking through my tears now, snivelling as my nasal passages filled up. I gulped in some air and resumed my stream of comforting words. He might not be able to hear but it made me feel better and it seemed to be keeping Rob grounded, too. Poor lad, losing his gran and then facing all this on the day of her funeral.

The ambulance arrived within ten minutes of the first call. The paramedics took over from Rob and me and congratulated us on stemming the blood loss from the wound. They took him out to their vehicle and spent some time checking his condition and ensuring that he was stable before setting off for the nearest A&E.

Rob and I followed in Owen's car. I had calmed down a bit once the paramedics took over, at least to the extent that I managed to stop crying, though I was still terrified. I kept reliving the moment when Ned had lunged towards Steve. It was lodged in my memory and kept replaying as if on a permanent loop.

I glanced at my watch and realised that this was the time we should have been setting out on our journey back to London – which immediately reminded me of work. I remembered that Steve had an important meeting in London the next day; that had been the reason for travelling home this afternoon. I needed to tell Barbara that he wouldn't make it and what was going on.

"Need to tell the office," I said to Rob in explanation. "Steve has a meeting tomorrow."

He nodded and smiled reassuringly. "I'm sure he'll be okay, Josh."

When the signal on my phone was strong enough, I dialled the office and got straight through to Barbara. There followed one of the most difficult phone conversations I'd ever had. By the end of it, if I'd ever doubted the closeness of the bond between Barbara and Steve, I certainly would never do so again. The poor woman was almost beside herself with grief and anxiety, and coping with her tears down the phone was bloody difficult. The lump in my throat felt so large I could barely get any words out at all.

Eventually I persuaded her that she needed to talk to Andy before he left the office for the day, and I promised to ring her again from the hospital as soon as there was any news. She said she would sort out some cover for Steve's meeting in the morning before she too headed north. I tried to dissuade her, but she insisted and I could understand why.

We arrived at the hospital and parked, then followed the signs for Casualty. Having been born and brought up in the area, Rob knew the layout of the building quite well, which helped considerably. We were directed to the waiting room by a rather stern, young receptionist. Being Steve's cousin, Rob was family so had some standing with the authorities. As a mere boyfriend I had no status, so Rob was asked to complete a questionnaire.

He grinned at me. "Steve and I were never that close," he said, "so you'll have to help me with this." It proved a welcome distraction and we filled in as much as we could. After handing it in, we were able to have words with a harassed-looking nurse.

"He recovered consciousness," he told us. "He seems to be doing okay. The doctor's with him now. We need to make sure that there's no internal bleeding, check that all his organs are intact and then monitor him for any sign of infection. If there's any sign of internal injury we might need to whip him into surgery, but we won't know for a while yet. The important thing is that there's no immediate danger. He should make a full recovery."

I breathed a huge sigh of relief. "Is he in pain?" I asked.

"I expect so but as soon as we know what's happening we can give him something for that. Whatever happens, he'll be very tired, so will need a good rest. It's pretty traumatic, getting stabbed like that." He dashed off, leaving us no alternative but to sit it out and hope for the best.

Owen joined us about half an hour later, having handed Ned over to his colleagues. As a witness to the incident he couldn't be the arresting officer, so he had left a statement and was then able to resume his day's leave. One of his colleagues from Skipton police station had given him a lift down to the hospital.

"Ned's being charged with attempted murder and GBH," he told us. "Other charges might follow, but the lads are keen to see him go down for a good long stretch."

"Good," I said.

Rob, on the other hand, was more sympathetic. "I don't know whether sending him to prison is really the answer. Watching him today, even though he was shouting and screaming, I couldn't help feeling that there's more to it, you know. I'd like to know more about his father's role. It was clear from what Ned said that his father forced him into giving evidence against Steve – how and why, I wonder? And why has Ned been so bitter and angry for all these years? There *has* to be more to it."

Owen smiled at his husband. "Trust you to side with the underdog, Rob – though I do see what you mean. There's definitely more to Ned's story than meets the eye. But the fact is that he was present when Jamie died, and he could have easily killed Steve this afternoon. That makes him a potential threat to us all."

It was another hour before anything happened. We sat in the waiting room and chatted or checked our phones. Eventually, a young man in a white coat appeared. He was smiling, which I took to be a good sign.

"Mr Bates?" he queried.

Rob smiled. "That's me."

"Some news of your cousin. So far as we can tell, the knife penetrated the abdomen but caused no damage internally. He is a very lucky man, I think. We need to keep him under observation for a couple of days in case there's any internal bleeding or signs of infection but if he's all clear, he can leave here the day after tomorrow."

Rob smiled at me. "How is he feeling?"

"A bit groggy and in some pain. But we can manage that for him now. Is one of you Josh?"

"That's me," I said.

"Well, he's quite anxious about you, Josh, and keeps asking for you. As soon as we've got him settled on a ward, you can go up and see him. Oh, and he mentioned some guy called Rhett as well."

I couldn't stop my face dissolving into a goofy grin. "Oh, that's me as well. Family joke. Thanks, I'll look forward to that."

As soon as he'd gone, I let out a big breath. Rob pulled me into a hug. "See?" he said with a big grin. "I told you he'd be all right. We've got tough hides in the Bates family."

"I'm making no comment whatever about that," said Owen, keeping a deadpan face.

All three of us burst out laughing as all the pent-up

tension of the last couple of hours drained away.

I pulled out my phone. "I must let Barbara know," I explained.

The Year of Awakening

Chapter 41

Steve

After blacking out in the pub, the next thing I remembered was being in the ambulance, but I was only conscious for a minute or two and then I faded out again.

The next thing I was aware of was lying on a bed alone in a cubicle somewhere. Judging by the smell and the noise going on outside, I was in a hospital, presumably in casualty.

The pain was excruciating – sharp and throbbing, like being hit repeatedly in the tummy by a baseball bat. Next thing I knew there was a guy standing next to me, looking over me anxiously.

"So you're back with us, then," he said with a gentle smile. "Hi. I'm Tariq and I'm looking after you. We need to run some checks on your wound before we can decide on the treatment you need. Once we know where we are, we can give you something for the pain. Does it hurt a lot?"

I nodded. "Certainly does," I replied, wincing as another baseball bat landed in my abdomen. "What sort of treatment?"

Tariq shrugged. "Depends on what shows up. If the knife damaged anything, you'll be suffering from internal bleeding and will need surgery to fix it. Other than that, the biggest risk is infection. We'll get you a CT scan as soon as possible and what we find on that will determine what we do next."

I must have passed out again, because the next thing I knew I was being wheeled on a trolley along endless corridors to get to the scanner. Once the scan was done, I was wheeled back to the ward and finally given some painkillers. These knocked me out again but not before I'd asked after Josh and the others.

When I awoke, something felt different. The pain was certainly less but there was something else. Then I realised what it was; my hand was being held, very tightly, by a rather attractive young man with chestnut hair who was smiling down at me.

His eyes were full of concern. When he realised I was awake, he leant down and brushed his lips over mine. "Hello, Steve," he said. "How are you doing?"

"Hurts like hell," I told him. "But otherwise okay, I think. It's been quite an afternoon, hasn't it? Are you all right?"

He nodded. "Feeling a lot better now we know you're not in any danger."

"Aren't I? Oh, good. The scan was okay, then?"

"Yeah, fine. Ned managed to miss everything important, apparently, so it's a matter of keeping you clear of infection and waiting for the wound to heal. You'll be laid up for a few weeks, I'm afraid. But we'll manage that – I've let Barbara know."

"Oh, shit. I've got that meeting in the morning, haven't I?"

"Don't worry, Andy and Luke have got it covered, and Andy has already spoken to the Griffin House people. You've got to focus on having a good rest and getting better."

I squeezed his hand. "Thanks, Josh, that's great. Have I mentioned that I love you?"

He grinned at me. "Not for a while but I think you've had other things on your mind today. Oh but, just for the record, I love you, too. Now you need some rest so we're going to leave you alone. I'll be back first thing in the morning. Barbara will be here by then as well."

He reached over and kissed me again. Rob and Owen said their goodnights. I lay back on the pillows, aware of little other than the dull ache in my midriff and how tired I felt. I wanted to try to process the events of the afternoon before I fell asleep again, but my eyelids drooped and I was away.

It was still dark when I was woken again to have my wound dressed and vital signs checked. More painkillers followed but I stayed awake for a while this time.

The last forty-eight hours had wrought a huge change in my life. I had begun to feel it the previous night, after reading Meg's letter, and it had now been confirmed by Ned – albeit unwillingly and in the most bizarre way.

Jamie's death was not suicide and therefore he had not broken his promise to me. I hadn't realised until I talked through everything with Josh the other week just how important that aspect of the whole trauma had been. I had coped with everything that those few terrible months had thrown at me – the arrest, the trial, and even the imprisonment – but what affected me most deeply was the sense of betrayal I had felt as a result of Jamie's alleged suicide. It was as if he had thrown away everything we had together; he had allowed his own short-term grief to outweigh the promises we'd made to and the future we were looking forward to. The fact that the last emotion I had felt towards the love of my life was anger and bitterness was almost too much to bear. I would never see him again. Was it the case that I would never think of him again without remembering that apparent betrayal?

The way I felt had coloured my life over the last twenty-one years. My reluctance to seek a new relationship, or even to indulge in a one-night stand, was driven by the bitterness I felt. The result had been a form of apathetic celibacy that had lasted until Josh breezed into my life and turned it upside down. It had been my strong feelings for him that had overcome everything else.

Now, the reason for my sense of betrayal had melted away. Jamie had not committed suicide, so had not broken his promise to wait for me. In fact, according to Ned, almost his last action had been to declare his love for me and refuse to betray it. That had been heroic – and might even have cost him his life.

For me, the result was the lifting of a burden on my shoulders that had seemed almost physical at times. Consequently, I had this sense of lightness, of walking on air. It had got me through the funeral service and helped me through the twin ordeals of returning to my home village and having to greet virtually the entire community at my aunt's funeral. I realised that it had even helped me during the exchange with Ned Hardwick. I'd had nothing to lose from confronting him – in fact, I had everything to gain. And it had proved to be the correct decision. I had got the confirmation that I had so desperately wanted, and it felt good.

I drifted off to sleep again.

When I awoke, it was light. Bright sunshine streamed through the windows of my room and it was several minutes before I was able to open my eyes fully. Josh was there to greet me and Barbara sat next to him. She was smiling, but her eyes were full of concern.

"Good morning, you two," I said, with a smile. "Been here long?"

"About half an hour," Josh said. "Barbara got here last night and stayed with Rob and Owen as well. Rob drove us into Skipton and I picked up a hire car this morning – we can't rely on them to transport us about all the time, they're busy chaps."

"Quite," I said. "What's the news – when can I go home?"

"In a couple of days, they think," replied Josh. "They need to make sure that you don't develop an infection and there is no internal bleeding. But getting the wound to heal fully is a long business, I'm afraid – two or three weeks minimum, they reckon."

I groaned. There was so much going on at the office and I needed to be there. "How come?

"Apparently, because the knife went quite deep, they're

using packing on the wound and that has to be monitored. The packing and the dressing have to be changed regularly, probably every couple of days. So we need to work out how we're going to cope with that and where you're going to be."

I groaned again.

Josh carried on. "I don't think my medical skills are up to the job, I'm afraid, even if I could prevent myself from keeling over if it started to bleed. So wherever you are, we need people to come in and look after you. Rob and Owen want us to stay with them. They think a local practice nurse would come in and look after your wound for as long as necessary."

"But what about work?"

Barbara intervened. "Josh will stay with you and act as your PA. He can work on the Griffin House project for next week and also be on hand to sort you out if any problems arise."

Josh grinned. "That way, I get to look after my hot boss without having to take any time off."

"Ah, I spy a cunning plan," I responded, about to laugh until I remember how much it would hurt. "No, seriously, it's a good plan, folks. Thanks." Then I remembered something. "But Josh you've got some more open-mike nights set up, haven't you?"

"There were a couple, yes, but I've already sorted them and rebooked them for later in the year. It's no big deal, honestly. Anyway, Ann and Gerry want me to go back and play at the White Horse," he added with a big grin. "So I'll at least keep my hand in."

The next couple of days in hospital dragged rather, aside

from the precious time that Josh spent with me. We talked about work for a while but also just chatted. Though we had established strong emotional bonds, we also had not had that much quality time together, time we could use to get to know each other properly. So we shared more family stuff, childhood memories, relationships with our parents, and personal likes and dislikes.

The other diversion during my hospital stay was the completion of witness statements about the stabbing. Inevitably this led on to my childhood memories of Ned Hardwick and, in particular, his relationship with Jamie. That was painful but much less so now than ever before. In talking about the past, I was once again reminded how much easier it felt having established the facts about Jamie's death.

After a couple of hours with the local detectives, I signed the statement. Now I could move on. They said that Ned had signed a full confession, so they expected him to plead guilty. It was unlikely that I would be called upon to repeat my statement in court. I was profoundly grateful and hoped Ned wouldn't change his mind.

The Year of Awakening

Chapter 42

Josh

Apart from visiting Steve in hospital, I spent some time getting to know his cousin Rob over the next couple of days. He and his husband Owen were very proud of their newly completed house and studio.

The latter impressed me hugely. Created at the barn end of the original building, the studio was an open space from floor to rafters, lit from above by skylights in the roof and by a huge window where the large barn door had once been. It was lavishly equipped with a control room, a high-tech sound system and something that made my eyes light up: a baby grand piano. In addition, there was enough floor space to accommodate a small ensemble of musicians.

"Wow," I breathed. "What a fantastic space."

Rob grinned. "Yeah, I am really pleased with it. It's been a lifelong ambition to have my own studio and I sometimes have to pinch myself when I come in here."

"Have you got lots of clients?"

"Several locally based musicians have come in and used

it for YouTube stuff and the word is spreading. People seem to love the space and the sound it creates. Maybe we should do some stuff with you while you're here."

"Really? That would be fantastic! I said to Steve the other week that I'd have to do some video and put it out there."

"Are you aiming for a full-time career, then?"

"To be honest, I'm not sure. I love being a consultant and working with Steve but I have this feeling that I was born to perform." I told him the sad story of dropping out of drama school and losing my confidence. Of not playing at all for three years.

"It was meeting Steve that did it," I added. "Whatever we've got together boosted my confidence so much – and he had just bought this amazing keyboard." I grinned. "I sat down to give it a try and everything just clicked. The feeling was amazing. It was as if I'd never stopped though I was terribly out of practice, of course."

Rob laughed. "You didn't sound out of practice in the White Horse yesterday afternoon. You made it very special, at least until Ned bloody Hardwick wrecked it all. But Meg would have so enjoyed hearing you play."

I felt myself blushing. "Thanks. It was good fun." I gave the baby grand a longing look. "May I?"

"Be my guest, Josh. It doesn't get played nearly enough."

I sat down and lifted the lid, running my fingers over the keyboard. "It's got a lovely tone," I said. "Did you get it new?"

Rob laughed and shook his head. "Good Lord, no. Couldn't run to that, I'm afraid. It's reconditioned, but it was a good make originally and they seem to have done a good refurb."

I moved from playing scales to a real tune and lost myself in a couple of George Gershwin numbers. At some point I heard the doorbell go and was aware that Rob had left the room. He returned a few minutes later with two women I vaguely recognised from the pub the previous afternoon. I stopped playing and stood up to greet them.

"Josh, this is Maggie and her wife, Diane. I don't think you were introduced yesterday."

I shook hands with them both. "So nice to meet you."

"We were on the way home and thought we'd just pop in to see what the news is about Steve," Maggie explained. She smiled at me. "I was Steve's best friend at junior school in Long Garfield ... too many years ago."

"And I'm a jazz music producer and wanted to hear you play again," Diane added.

I stood there amazed, my mouth opening and closing, not knowing what to say. Eventually, I managed, "Gosh."

"I had only just arrived yesterday when you played your last number – and then, of course, everything fell apart, so I didn't get the chance to introduce myself," she explained.

"Well, there's no time like the present," I said, resuming my seat on the piano stool.

Rob waved Maggie and Diane to a sofa and I picked up the Gershwin where I left off. I finished that number, and then did a couple more of my own favourites, including my 'theme tune' of 'Luck Be a Lady'.

As I finished, the three of them applauded loudly, making me blush once more.

Diane was really buzzing. "Josh, that was wonderful," she said. "What have you been doing with all this talent?"

For the second time that afternoon, I told my story, and

how I'd only recently started playing again.

"Have you done any gigs?" Diane asked.`

"So far, just the one open-mike night at the Flying Pig in Lewisham last week," I told her. "It went really well."

"Good. It's a great venue. I'm not surprised it went well if you played and sang like that. I'll bet you brought the house down," she responded. "Tell me, have you signed up with anybody? Record label, agent, anyone?"

I shook my head. "I haven't had the chance yet. I'm not entirely sure where all this is going and I haven't really thought about what I want out of it," I explained.

"For what it's worth, Josh, I think you should definitely pursue it. You clearly have a great talent. Have you got some videos online yet?"

"Rob and I were just talking about that," I said. "As I'm going to be here with Steve for a couple of weeks, I could record some stuff if Rob's got the time."

Diane nodded. "Great idea." She turned to Rob. "Had you thought of involving Gavin and Ben?"

Rob opened his eyes wide. "Diane, that's a brilliant idea." He turned to me. "Gavin Parker and Ben Kennedy live up the road. Gavin plays bass and Ben the drums. If they're not on the road, I'm sure they'd love to come and play with you."

"That sounds great," I responded. "I've always wanted to have a go as part of a trio."

"Right. Let's see what I can set up." Rob disappeared to the phone whilst I chatted with Maggie and Diane. The pair of them were great fun and I really enjoyed their company.

Maggie said she would pop in again when Steve was

home from hospital. Diane made me promise to keep in touch. "See if you can get a good session in the can," she said. "Then let me have a copy and I'll see what I can do to set you up with some gigs." She paused and then smiled. "We'll have you playing the Albert Hall before you know it."

I laughed at that. "As if."

"Well, you never know," she responded, as they headed out of the house to their car.

I picked up Steve from hospital the next day. He looked a lot better but was still in considerable pain from the wound. Manoeuvring to get him in the car so that he could be comfortable for the journey was a bit of a challenge, but we managed to get him in a sort of half-lying position in the back seat so that we minimised the pressure on his wound.

He looked very tired when we got back to the house after the forty-five minute drive. I got him inside, only to find myself wrapped in a big hug.

"I've been wanting to hold you for three days," he said. "And now I've got you, I've barely got the energy to stand up."

"Well, let's not then," I replied. "Come on, we'll get you horizontal and then I can give you a proper cuddle. Cuddles are my speciality, if you remember."

He grinned at me. "How could I forget?"

Ten minutes later, we lay on the bed in our room entwined in each other's arms, carefully arranged so as to keep clear of Steve's stomach.

Suddenly, he gave a huge yawn. "You wouldn't believe that a fit and healthy man could be laid so low by one wound," he said. "I'm bloody exhausted and I haven't done anything except ride in a car for three-quarters of an hour."

"It's the shock," I replied. "Plus the fact that you've stopped. It's been a pretty intensive few months, one way and another. I think you were more tired than you realised."

"You're probably right." He grinned at me. "It's your fault, of course. You've worn me out with your amorous desires."

"Oh, sure. Like you didn't have any at all," I countered.

"Me? No, no. I was just an innocent."

"Yeah, yeah. I really buy that!" I laughed. "Anyway, you'll have a chance to recover over the next two weeks, since you're banned from doing *anything* until you've healed up."

Steve groaned. "I choose this moment to fall for the hottest boy on the planet, then get myself stabbed so that I can't do anything about it."

I laughed. "Thank you for the compliment. Flattery will get you everywhere. Just think how good it will be when you're fully recovered. Talk about twice nightly."

"I can't wait." He kissed me lightly, which felt wonderful, then relaxed back onto the pillows. I held him until he dozed off and felt myself nodding too. It was blissful to have him back.

✦

I slept for about an hour and woke up with my arms still round Steve. He had not moved at all and was still fast asleep. Needing the bathroom, I disengaged myself from him without waking him and got up.

Leaving the bathroom, I went downstairs. Rob had just got home from a meeting and Owen was cooking.

"How's the patient?" Rob asked with a smile.

"Fast asleep. He was completely whacked when we got back from the hospital, so he's been asleep for about an hour. I thought I'd take him some tea in a minute, if that's okay."

"Sure, no problem," Owen said, reaching for the kettle. "Supper will be about an hour. Presumably Steve won't come down?"

I shook my head. "I think the wound needs to heal a bit more. Travelling home took such a lot out of him. I was quite shocked, really – and so was he, I think."

Owen nodded. "I can understand that. I was injured in a bike accident a while back. Nothing major, but it took me far longer to get over it than I expected. I think it's the shock as much as anything else."

"Anyway," I said. "We're both really grateful that we could stay with you for a while. I'm sure it'll be better for him than London, even if he was fit to travel all that way."

"Aye, lad, a good bit of Yorkshire air," Rob said with a laugh. "Besides we've got to get these recordings done before you can leave."

"Any news on Ben and Gavin?" I asked.

"Oh, sorry, I forgot. Ben called a while ago. He'd picked up my message. They'd love to come and talk about it, get to know you. They'll be here on Wednesday morning, if that's okay."

"More than," I responded with a grin. "I shall really look forward to that."

Steve had just woken up when I took him his tea. He looked adorable with his long hair tousled on the pillow. Having put his cup down on the bedside table, I sat on the edge of the bed. He moved over a little to make room for me and I reached out to stroke his hair, pushing it away from his face.

"Hey there, sleepyhead. How are you doing?" I asked.

"Feeling a lot better. Only moderately knackered now instead of completely exhausted," he said, with a short laugh.

"Good," I responded. "Hungry?"

He thought for a moment. "I could certainly manage a little something."

"Great. Owen's cooking and it should be ready in about an hour. I'll bring you some up."

Steve tried to sit up to drink his tea, then winced with pain and sank bank. "God this is going to be bloody tedious," he remarked. He rested for a few moments before I helped him to sit more upright. His phone buzzed at that moment and he picked the call up.

"Hi, Andy. How's things?"

It was Andy Pearson, calling for an update. I left Steve to it and headed back downstairs, smiling to myself. Something told me I was going to get to know these stairs rather well over the next couple of weeks.

Chapter 43

Steve

It was good to catch up with Andy and particularly to get his reassurance that everything was fine in my absence.

"We need you to get yourself better, not worry so much that you have a relapse," he said firmly. He was echoing Barbara's words but they helped me to relax a little. He and Barbara were both adamant that the business wouldn't collapse in my absence. After all, as the old adage had it, nobody is truly indispensable.

After Andy hung up, I lay back on the pillows, exhausted by the effort required to do a simple thing like answer the phone. It seemed ridiculous, but it was the way the body reacted to the shock of a wound like mine and there was nothing I could do about it. The doctor had told me that my generally high fitness levels meant that I should recover more quickly than average. That was some consolation, I supposed.

I must have dozed again because it hardly seemed two minutes before Josh came back into the room with some supper on a tray.

"Hey, sleepyhead," he said. "Supper's up."

"Bless you – I hadn't realised how hungry I was until I smelt the food as you came upstairs."

Josh put down the tray and helped manoeuvre me into a sitting position that was not too uncomfortable. As he did so, his hand brushed my cheek. I caught his fingers in mine and lifted them to my lips. "You look after me so well, Rhett," I told him with a smile.

He grinned down. "Why thank you, Miss Scarlett. It's my pleasure. Now, come on. Eat up before it gets cold."

As the next couple of days passed, I started to feel better. The nurse came in to change my dressing a couple of times; the second time, she announced that we could dispense with the packing, which was really good news. It meant that I was making progress and it made things much less uncomfortable.

On Wednesday morning, Rob's friends Ben and Gavin arrived and spent the morning in the studio with Josh. From what I could hear, the three of them established an immediate rapport. Not only were the sounds drifting upstairs to my bedroom from the studio impressive, I could hear that the room was full of laughter as well as music. I smiled to myself, pleased for Josh, but it added to my frustration at having to stay in bed for a few more days.

As I lay back on the pillows, I couldn't help but feel a little uncertain about the pace of events. In a year when so much in my life had changed, another shift was occurring beneath my feet. Excited as I was for Josh, I was not altogether sure that I was ready for what might happen next.

The man himself emerged from the session with a wide grin on his face. He announced that the three of them had arranged with Rob to film a session the following week.

"It was fantastic, Steve. We just clicked. Ben and Gavin are already talking about us to doing a tour together." Josh was unable to keep the excitement out of his voice. "That's if Diane could get us some dates."

I smiled with him and made enthusiastic noises, but all the time I could hear Barbara's words at the pub in Lewisham the previous week: "You'll lose him now." I shivered with fear at the recollection, just as I had that night.

I looked up to find Josh looking at me intently. He smiled gently and spoke quietly. "Remember, Steve. You're my rock."

Christ, how does he do that? It was as if he could read my mind.

Josh laughed. "Don't worry. I'm not a mind reader. I don't need to be because I can see it all in your eyes. I know that you sometimes feel abandoned – that everybody important in your life has gone away and left you. But, as I told you last week, you're lumbered with me. Just don't spoil our happiness by worrying all the time that it's not going to last."

"Objectively, I know you're right. Of course you are – and please don't think it's because I don't trust you," I replied. "It's just sometimes a shadow of doubt crosses my mind..."

He nodded. "I know what you mean. Every now and

again, in the middle of the night, I hear Greg's voice again telling me that I'm no good and I can't do this. To give up and stay indoors." As he said spoke, his expression darkened. Then his face cleared just as quickly and he grinned at me. "Then I have days like today, when I know bloody well I can. Then I feel on top of the world."

Chapter 44

Josh

I worked hard between meeting Ben and Gavin for that first session and the recording session. Obviously I needed to keep practising, which I did each morning for a couple of hours, then there was looking after Steve and keeping him on the road to recovery. I had help from the nurses who came in to check his dressings, and the running up and downstairs got less as he recovered steadily – especially now he was allowed to get up for a couple of hours every day

I was also acting as Steve's PA for the stuff that Andy and Barbara were referring to him. Fortunately they were dealing with as much as possible themselves but they needed Steve's guidance on his own project work and on some of the business-wide issues. We agreed to spend at least an hour a day on that but in practice it usually took less.

What I loved was the fact that we seemed to grow even closer as the time went on. We shared a bed at night but I was also having to help him with shaving and showering. If we had been close and emotionally involved before Meg's funeral, we were certainly very intimate now; if our lives had been converging before, they were now positively intertwined.

My only fear was what would happen when we got back to London. Would we revert to our previous lives, with me spending most weekday nights in my own room at Robbie and Malcolm's place? I was not sure that I wanted to sleep alone at night any more. I'd miss the physical proximity, the jokes, the comfort of Steve's presence in my life and in bed beside me.

On the other hand, I didn't know whether Steve was ready for such a big step as moving in together – especially as somebody who had been alone and independent for so many years.

In the end, I told myself that there was no point in second-guessing the situation. We'd see what happened when we got him home to Crystal Palace and settled back in the flat. Meanwhile, there was the video recording session to do and the enormous fun of making music with Ben and Gavin.

When the day came, it went amazingly well. We'd agreed that we'd try for the three tracks in my open-mike set to release first. It made sense, because those three were firmly in my mind and, when we put them on the internet, they would be familiar to audiences who'd seen me live. Diane came in for the recording and sat on the sofa at one end of the studio with Steve. They'd promised faithfully to be as quiet as mice, and so they were.

In the event, things went so smoothly that we quickly rehearsed and then recorded another two tracks – another

Gershwin number, 'But Not For Me,' and the poignant Rodgers and Hart number 'Ev'ry Time We Say Goodbye'. We all knew and loved the famous Ella Fitzgerald recording of the song and paying tribute to it seemed to be a great idea.

When we wrapped up, all three of us had grins on our faces almost as wide as the room. Diane was shaking her head with wonder. "I cannot believe that you've only played together twice," she told us. "It sounds as if you've worked with one another for years."

Rob came into the room then, having quickly reviewed the takes to make sure everything was okay. He gave us the thumbs up. "Looks and sounds really great," he said. "I'll get them edited and ready to upload, then let you all review them."

Steve had remained on the sofa, firmly in the background. I went over and joined him. "That sounded really great," he said, with a big smile. "We'll have you at Ronnie Scott's yet."

"Oh, I don't know about that," I responded with a laugh. "I was thinking more of the Royal Albert Hall!"

"Well, we might manage the Albert Halls in Bolton," Diane intervened. "But I think the London one might be a bit out of our reach."

I grinned. "I'll settle for Bolton for the time being – but trust me the London one won't be far behind."

"There's nothing like having ambition," Rob intervened. "Just so long as I get to be there recording it!"

Steve stayed up for the whole of that day, the first time he had done so since coming home from hospital, so by the time we went upstairs he was exhausted. As I helped him get ready for bed, he leaned in and kissed me.

"What was that for, Mr Frazer?"

"I was so proud of you today. I sat there listening to you play and sing, all confident and full of beans, and remembered the tentative way you started that Sunday in the flat. You've come such a long way, Josh."

"Gosh, yes. I remember that day. When you showed me your machine and I just had to play it." I grinned again and waggled my eyebrows at him.

Steve laughed. "But seriously, though. I knew as soon as you started how talented you were and then when you used to practise on those Sunday mornings. Somehow today, listening to the three of you, it moved to a new dimension."

I couldn't help blushing slightly. "You're right – it certainly is a whole new ball game, playing with two others. But it's great. I find that it sharpens my reactions, because I have to really listen to what the other two are doing and react to it. It gives me an incredible buzz."

Suddenly Steve gave the most tremendous yawn. "I'm sorry, Josh. I really am absolutely done tonight."

I wrapped my arms about him carefully, trying to avoid his tender areas. "Say good night then, Scarlett. Sleep tight."

He responded with a kiss on the forehead then smiled. "Night, Rhett."

He was asleep before I could get his head down on the pillow.

Chapter 45

Steve

The next two weeks passed amazingly quickly, considering I actually did very little. This was the first extended break I'd taken since helping to found Pearson Frazer five years earlier and, to my surprise, I rather enjoyed it. It was the company that made the difference, of course. The weather helped as well as we enjoyed two weeks of glorious July sunshine.

We fell into a routine of lazy breakfasts then spent an hour keeping up with e-mails and other company matters, though in truth the tasks took less time than that on many days. Once I was able to go out, we walked in the garden for a while before lunch. As I got fitter, the walks got longer and strayed further from the house.

After a doze after lunch, I spent the afternoon reading while Josh worked on establishing his social media presence, setting up pages and then posting stuff on them. Rob had turned the videos round and put the first of them up on the web, and the trio had agreed on a schedule for the release of the others at monthly intervals in the run up to Christmas. A further session was scheduled for the autumn to record some Christmas tracks.

Rob and Owen were wonderful hosts. The trauma of the funeral and its aftermath meant that the four of us had forged a strong emotional bond. Those two weeks of recuperation helped cement that into a lifelong friendship.

Josh played two more sessions at the White Horse down in Long Garfield, and we had a couple of great evenings with Ann and Gerry and the pub regulars, as I laughed and swapped anecdotes with old and new friends in the village.

Those two evenings provided great memories for me to store up and helped change my perception of the village where I'd grown up. I could now look back on those years without summoning up a whole series of unhappy ghosts. I could never forget the pain of my arrest and Jamie's death, and I would always mourn him, but the memories were now less searing than they had been before I had met Josh. The events of twenty-one years ago no longer defined me, and they no longer cast a shadow over the rest of my life. It was a welcome change.

However, all good things must come to an end, and my check-up with the hospital at the end of the second week gave me the all-clear to return to London. I could resume full-time work a week after that. Our little Yorkshire idyll was over.

We arranged to head south on the following Monday. Rob and Owen insisted on cooking a farewell lunch for us on Sunday and hurriedly convened a party comprising Ben, Gavin, Maggie and Diane. We had a riotous afternoon; the air was full of laughter and joking, anecdotes and memories. Inevitably, we ended up in the studio as Ben,

Gavin and Josh made music together and the rest of us did our best to help by singing along.

I started to fade around five. Josh took me off upstairs, which was the cue for the other four guests to take their leave. After settling me down, he headed downstairs to help Rob and Owen with the clearing up.

As I lay there, something was nagging at me, preventing me from relaxing fully. After a few minutes, it dawned on me what it was: going back to London meant that the time that Josh and I had spent together was coming to an end as well. He would almost certainly be going back to his room with Robbie and Malcolm for several nights a week, as he had in the weeks before Meg's death.

I realised how much I would miss him if that happened. The weeks since Meg's funeral had definitely wrought a change in our relationship and drawn us even closer together. I could not now imagine my life without Josh in it; it was time to tell him, and to ask him to move in with me.

Having reached that decision, I fell asleep. I awoke around three-quarters of an hour later, to find the object of my affections smiling down at me.

"I brought you a cuppa," he said. "I figured you wouldn't want to sleep too long."

I stretched luxuriously, bringing myself to full consciousness. "Thanks, Rhett. That's mighty kind of you."

"Are you okay?" he asked.

"Yeah. More than okay, actually. I reached a decision before I went to sleep and I want to run something by you." I made room for him and patted the side of the mattress.

"Come and sit for a minute."

Josh looked puzzled but then complied.

I paused for a moment then spoke again. "I realised earlier that when we got back to London, you'd probably go back to Robbie and Malcolm's – at least for some nights a week. And I realised how much I didn't want that to happen. How much I wanted you in my life all the time."

Josh's eyes widened and the sides of his mouth started to turn up, giving me the courage to carry on.

"So, I was thinking that you might like to throw in your lot with me full time."

"Live with you? All the time? Me?"

I nodded.

"Gosh, Steve!"

He paused. I closed my eyes for a moment, steeling myself for some form of rejection or gentle put down. Then I opened them quickly, to see a big smile spread across his face. "That's fantastic. I'd been thinking the same thing, about missing you. So I'd love to. But on one condition: that you let me pay my way."

"But..."

"Yes, I know it might not be strictly necessary, but I must support myself in some way or another. I can't – and won't let myself be – *totally* dependent, like I was on Greg. I love you very much, Steve, and I want to spend the rest of my life with you. And I know that you're not Greg, but...'

I nodded. "I totally get that, Josh. Don't worry, we'll work something out. Have a joint account and both contribute, or something. But if that's the only problem..."

He nodded and suddenly we were in each other's arms.

"There you are," I said, resting my forehead on his.

"Sealed with a kiss."

The Year of Awakening

Chapter 46

Josh

As we sat on the bed cuddling after our decision to move in together, I realised that it was time to make another decision. "Whilst we're on the subject of change, there's something else we need to talk about," I said. "My future with Pearson Frazer."

"Oh?"

"Yeah. Diane was saying this afternoon that an autumn tour is a serious possibility. Rob says the YouTube numbers are approaching half a million. That means it's possible we'd have some sort of fan base on which to launch ourselves."

A look of pure joy lit up Steve's face. "Josh, that's fantastic news. I had no idea things had moved that quickly. Why didn't you say anything earlier?"

"I just wanted to absorb it, to think it through. But it's pretty clear that if I'm going to pursue music, I can't hold down a full-time job as well."

Steve nodded. "No, I understand that. We've talked about it before, and I think Barbara is resigned to it."

"Yeah, you said the other week."

"But I have a possible solution that doesn't involve you cutting ties altogether."

I gazed at Steve intently. "And?"

"Well, to be frank, I – in fact all of us at the firm – don't want to lose you. Andy particularly is really keen to keep you on in some form or other. He suggested you could come on our books as a freelancer."

I frowned. "How would that work?"

"Well, you'd give us a schedule of your availability and we'd agree a set of tasks that you could complete – it might be project work, or working on a bid, like we did with Griffin House, or just business development. But we'd guarantee to buy whatever time you were prepared to offer us for a fixed period – say a year. If your music career takes off and you don't have any time, we wouldn't buy any."

"Steve! That's amazing. Are you sure?"

"Not my idea, Josh. As I say, it came from Andy and I'm sure Barbara will agree – in fact I know she will. We don't want to lose you."

"I don't know what to say – it sounds too good to be true. I'd love that."

We headed downstairs after that and joined Rob and Owen for a bite of supper and a farewell drink. Rob was clearly on edge and I could see that he was trying to pluck up the courage to ask Steve something.

Eventually, during a lull in the conversation, he took a deep breath and spoke. "Er, Steve. Before you go back off to London, I – we – that is some people in the village and us – wanted to ask a favour. We want to found a charity in Meg's name and wondered whether you'd agree to be involved."

"What would the charity do?"

"Try to help look after LGBT youth," he replied, still clearly anxious about the idea and what impact it might have on Steve. "We thought it would be the right thing. It was a subject very close to Meg's heart after what happened to you and Jamie, and then with me being gay."

"That sounds a terrific idea," Steve responded, cocking an eyebrow at me and getting a short nod in return. "Count me in."

"Oh, fantastic!"

"Me too," I chipped in. "From all you said at the funeral, she was a very special lady."

"Yeah, she was," Owen intervened. "She used to worry so much about the gay kids in the area, where they went, and so on."

Rob laughed. "Do you remember that family in the village who threw their boy out when he was caught kissing his friend?"

"Do I ever?" Owen responded. "I'll never forget the look on Meg's face when I told her what was going on."

Rob turned to us. "Gran marched round to the house and banged on the door so loudly you could hear it three streets away. She berated the two parents for at least twenty minutes ... and wouldn't leave until they agreed to take the boy back. There was Gran, five foot nothing, yelling at this bloke who was almost two feet taller and twice as wide. She just stood her ground. It was amazing."

"I can just imagine it. I only ever crossed swords with her once," Steve replied with another bark of laughter. "The tongue-lashing I got convinced me that it wasn't worth the candle arguing with her."

"Oh, I learned that at a very early age," Rob replied, still with laughter in his voice.

"Anyway, Rob. Count us in – we'll do whatever we can when you need us," Steve told his cousin.

Once upstairs, Steve and I spent a few minutes packing our stuff ready for departure in the morning before going to bed and wrapping ourselves in each other's arms.

"I shall miss this room," Steve said, with a gentle smile.

"You've certainly spent a good few hours in here over the past couple of weeks."

"And now I've been declared fit, I can make mad, passionate love to you as well," Steve responded with a grin.

"Why that sounds a mighty fine idea," I responded. "Mighty fine. Y'all want any help with that?"

Suddenly, the mood shifted and Steve's expression turned serious. "Yes, actually, you can help, Josh. I'd like you to be the top tonight."

"Gosh, Steve. Are you sure? I mean last time, even when it was accidental, you said..."

Steve nodded. "Yeah, I know what I said. But that was then and this is now, Josh. So much has happened over the last few weeks and months, and things have changed. I'm ready for this, and I want to make the final connection. I want you to claim me."

I gulped slightly. It was a long time since I'd been a top, and it had never happened all that often, especially not with Greg, who always wanted to be in charge. But I realised that this meant that I'd never really made *love* to anybody – and that was very different from a quickie on a college hook-up.

I smiled at him. "Of course I will. I should be honoured to," I replied and then kissed him, gently at first but with increasing fervour.

What followed was one of the most passionate and memorable nights of my life. When eventually we climaxed together, it was the most intense orgasm I had ever experienced, even after continually scaling the heights of what seemed possible during my few months with Steve.

The Year of Awakening

Chapter 47

Steve

Despite my resolve – my intense need – to feel Josh inside me, I was nervous about how my body would react to such an invasion, and whether my instinctive reaction in pushing Josh away a few months ago would recur. With hindsight, it was not surprising, given all that had happened in prison all those years ago – and then, of course, it had been followed by some twenty years of complete celibacy.

But, as I had said to Josh, my life had changed so much over the last few months, and the ending of the long nightmare of Jamie's death had undoubtedly had a profound effect on everything – an effect I had yet to process fully.

My need for Josh in this way had only arisen since the revelations at the funeral, which was why I felt that things would be okay. And, of course, it helped that Josh was so loving and careful in preparing me. As a result, when he entered me it was a natural progression of an act of love and felt nothing like the alien invasion I had endured as a young man.

Josh made love to me beautifully, with the perfect

combination of gentleness and mastery. He brought us to a simultaneous conclusion that left me wondering what had hit me. Afterwards, we lay side by side, gradually recovering both our breath and our equilibrium. I could only manage one word. "Wow," I said.

Josh grinned at me. "Wow indeed. God, I love you Steven Frazer. That was so ... amazing."

"And I love you too," I responded. "I am so lucky to have found you. I bless the day you walked into that interview room last July."

Josh gave a small laugh. "Even if you did try to frighten me off. Damn near succeeded at one point, too."

"I know. Don't remind me, please."

"Anyway, it all turned out okay in the end."

I reached up and stroked the side of his face. "More than okay. And I've now got my forever moment as well, even if I did have to wait more than twenty years for it."

"Well, we've got the rest of our lives to make up for lost time," Josh replied, kissing the hand I had used to stroke his cheek. "So on a practical note, we'd better start by cleaning ourselves up and getting some sleep, otherwise we'll never get up for the train in the morning."

He fetched a damp cloth and towel, and cleaned me up gently, as if I were a fragile piece of china. It was a blissful sensation and added to the overwhelming feeling of contentment that was stealing up on me.

I kissed my beautiful boyfriend goodnight and composed myself for sleep. Our arms and legs entwined. Just before I drifted off, I remembered my fears that day when I first laid eyes on him. Looking at him that day, I had felt instinctively that he would turn my life upside down. On the whole, that was a pretty accurate appraisal. What I hadn't expected was that the experience would be so enjoyable or have every prospect of lasting for the rest of my life. Josh had woken me from my long ordeal; for that alone, he deserved my undying love.

The Year of Awakening

Epilogue

Twelve Months Later

Josh

"Do I really have to get up on stage?" grumbled Steve. "Couldn't Rob do it?"

"I'll be too busy doing the recordings, I'm afraid," Rob responded.

"No, Steve. It's down to you, old chap." I intervened. "All you've got to do is thank everybody for coming, thank the performers and announce how much money we've raised."

We were in the final stages of preparing for our benefit concert for the Meg's Charity, the organisation we'd helped Rob to found the previous autumn in memory of his mother. I would be playing, together with Ben and Gavin, as the Josh Ashcroft Trio. Other local artists were also taking part. We were performing in Settle, just up the road from Meg's home village of Long Garfield and had come up to stay for a few days with Rob and Owen. It was the first time we'd been back since the funeral and its aftermath.

Getting Steve up on stage was an essential feature of my secret plan for the night, and I had enlisted Rob's help to make sure it happened. He and Owen were fully prepared to persuade Steve that he really did have to do this. He'd been muttering and grumbling about this ever since I'd mentioned it in the car on the way up.

"Anyway," I said, "you're well used to all that stuff. Think of all the presentations you do and conferences you speak at."

"I know but this feels different. More personal. Closer to home. I don't know. I just wish I didn't have to do it."

He looked at me and stuck out his bottom lip in a perfect imitation of a six-year-old pouting. Once he started joking, I knew it would be all right.

He grinned at me. "Don't worry, I'll put on my best professional Pearson Frazer voice and be authoritative."

I laughed. "That's the idea. You'll wow them with your eloquence."

I grinned at Rob and then relaxed a little. That had been a tense moment. A year into our relationship, I had fathomed most of Steve's moods and reactions. I tried to make life as easy as possible for him. His physical and mental recovery from the traumas of last summer had generally been good, and in particular there had been no major meltdown in the office. Both Barbara and I worked hard to ensure that he stayed calm, both for the sake of his blood pressure, and for the other staff. After all, I knew only too well what it was like to be on the receiving end of one of his rants.

Meanwhile, he and I had grown steadily closer; our

personal chemistry remained strong and our love for each other had deepened. I could not imagine a time or an existence without Steve in my life. Time spent away from each other was definitely not fun, and nights not sleeping in his arms were torture.

The Josh Ashcroft Trio had gone from strength to strength, with hefty viewing and follower numbers on social media. We had toured the previous autumn and played to an average of seventy-five-per-cent-full houses – not bad for an ensemble that had not existed until last June.

My switch to freelance working had gone very smoothly and proved invaluable. Ben and Gavin had other commitments so could not commit to the trio full time and, to be honest, I wasn't sure that I wanted to either. Extensive touring was exhausting and would take me away from Steve for too many nights. Continuing to work part time as a consultant kept me grounded and stimulated. It was also great to watch the firm grow from strength to strength on the back of the Griffin House project and other work won whilst I was away the previous autumn.

Steve and Andy were recruiting again and the following week they were due to interview a boy from my old university. He'd been a year behind me on the same course and I thought very highly of him.

"Time to go, I think," said Owen, breaking my line of thought. "Everybody ready?"

The three of us chorused a 'yes' and headed for the door. It was a perfect June evening, and my breath was once again taken away by the view from the front of Rob and Owen's property. Tonight, the heat and stillness of the day had resulted in a slight haze over everything, so the view of the Lakeland hills to the north was rather obscured. Even so, the outlook was spectacular and was accompanied by a veritable chorus of birdsong, led by a particularly vociferous blackbird.

Steve's voice broke my reverie. "Come on, Josh. Jump in, otherwise we'll all be late."

"What? Oh, sorry – it's the view. I was transfixed there for a moment." I shook my head to clear it and then clambered into Owen's SUV. We set off for Settle.

The hall was a sell-out, so the atmosphere by the time we got on stage was electric. We'd been pretty much guaranteed a full house: as well as Meg's reputation locally, loads of people in the hall knew our drummer Ben and bass player Gavin, and of course Rob and Owen were well known throughout the area.

Ben, Gavin and I stood at the side of the stage, ready to take our places on stage. I grinned at the other two and nodded. We walked on to thunderous applause and took our places. After a moment to settle down, I counted the guys in to what had become our standard opening number, 'Fly Me to the Moon'. We were off.

Steve

It was a great evening; the audience was responsive and appreciative, and all the artists responded well, revelling in the atmosphere. The trio was playing their second encore, but I knew this would definitely be their last number – apart from anything else, they were all starting to look tired, which wasn't surprising after nearly an hour and three-quarters on stage.

I prepared to do my bit and moved from the auditorium through to the wings, nodding and smiling in response to a whispered 'break a leg' from Owen. Somebody handed me a radio mike and, as the boys reached their final chords, I moved on to the stage and spoke.

"Ladies and gentlemen, the Josh Ashcroft Trio!"

The applause was thunderous and there were whistles and hollering as well. God, no wonder artists got hooked on applause.

I let the crowd carry on for a while and then held my hand up as a signal for quiet. "I won't keep you long, but I just wanted to say a big thank you to the trio and to all our guests tonight for a great show, and for coming along to support Meg's Charity. My aunt was a very special lady, and I'm sure she would have loved tonight's performance, as well as all the work amongst young LGBT people that we're able to do as a result of your generosity. So thank you for coming. I'm pleased to announce that we've raised the sum of £10,500 tonight, which is a really great result."

I was about to sign off when my eye caught a movement to my right.

Josh unhooked his microphone from the stand. "Ladies and Gentlemen, just before you go, there is one more thing I want to do tonight."

I looked up at him in puzzlement as he rose from his place on the piano stool and came to the front of the stage. Was he planning a duet or something?

"In a couple of weeks, it will be two years since I turned up at the offices of a leading environmental consultancy for a job interview and met this man here. We did not exactly hit it off at first but that changed as we worked together and got to know each other."

He paused for breath and glanced at me with a wicked grin on his face. "In fact, it turned out that we got on very well indeed – so much so that he turned from rather scary boss into the man of my dreams."

There was a collective 'ah' from the audience. Suddenly, I knew what was going to happen and began to blush furiously.

Josh turned from the audience to face me and looked me directly in the eye. "Steve Frazer, I love and respect you beyond all words. You gave me the courage to follow my dream of performing and you have transformed my existence for the better in so many ways. I want so very much to spend the rest of my life with you..."

Suddenly we lost eye contact and I realised that he had gone down on one knee and reached into his pocket for a small box. "Will you marry me?"

My eyes filled with tears and I could barely speak. I nodded vigorously, then managed to find some sort of voice and had the presence of mind to speak into the microphone. "I'd be honoured to."

Josh put the ring on my finger and rose, stepping into my embrace. We kissed and the applause once again drowned out all other noise so that I had to get really close to his ear. "You devil. I'll get you for this, Rhett Butler."

He grinned. "You said 'yes.' That's all that matters. As for the rest, well ... frankly my dear, I don't give a damn."

Epilogue

Acknowledgements

My grateful thanks to my editor Karen Holmes, proof reader Jamie Anderson and cover designer Hilary Pitts for their hard work in helping to bring this book to market. My deepest thanks also to my husband Michael Anderson and to all my friends for their help and encouragement over the last few months.

About the Author

Chris Cheek was born and brought up in South London. He has strong family ties with northern England and is a graduate of Lancaster University. He and his husband, Michael, have been together for forty years and have lived in the Yorkshire Dales since 1994.

This is Chris's second novel. His first book, *The Stamp of Nature*, was published in June 2018.

He writes a regular blog which can be found at www.chrischeek.me.

"A fascinating, intriguing, bittersweet, poignant, honest, blunt, emotionally charged, and interesting story that caught my attention from beginning to end."

THE
STAMP
OF
NATURE

Chris Cheek

Reviewers' verdicts on Chris Cheek's first novel, published in June 2018.

"A well-crafted tale of homophobia, the fear it creates, and the long lasting effects from it"

Growing up gay in 1960s Britain, facing prejudice and discrimination as students and later as teachers - against the background of a battle over reforms at an old-fashioned school. Who will win and how will it affect everybody's lives?

"a beautiful glimpse of a bygone era".
"a fascinating insight on some of the immense struggles that took place"

Still available in print and ebook format

See **www.chrischeek.me** for more details.

Lightning Source UK Ltd.
Milton Keynes UK
UKHW021941191118
332600UK00014B/1477/P